"AREN'T YOU EVEN GOING TO TRY?"

"You want me to seduce you?"

"Sure." Tori couldn't believe she said that. But hadn't she expected something of the sort when she'd agreed to come to the Keys with him? She wasn't naive. She knew that when the very air between a man and a woman sizzled, passion was inevitable. Wasn't it time for her to be honest with herself?

"If that's what you want. . . ." He dropped his feet to the floor and disappeared up the winding staircase to the loft on the second level.

She heard the rasp of a zipper and shivered in anticipation. How had she ever thought of Matt as serious and stodgy?

Moments later when he fully rounded the last curve of the stairway, she saw that he was holding two silver candlesticks that he'd packed in his suitcase.

MARILYN FORSTOT
Sunshine Riches

ZEBRA BOOKS
KENSINGTON PUBLISHING CORP.

ZEBRA BOOKS

are published by

Kensington Publishing Corp.
475 Park Avenue South
New York, NY 10016

First Printing: February, 1993

Printed in the United States of America

To the Thursday group: Friends, mentors, teachers. Audrey Austin, Helen Barkdohl, Kate Higuera, Sharon Ihle, Judi Lind, Diana Saenger, Jan Toom, Billie Wade.

And Marge Campbell.

Thank you.

Prologue

Large warm drops of Florida rain dappled Victoria's shoulders as she dashed for her car. Within moments her usually tidy chignon was clinging to her nape like seaweed. She tugged at the lapel of her suit jacket, pulling it tighter over the multiple listing book she hugged protectively against her chest.

As she climbed into the car, she put the real estate volume on the seat beside her, relieved that the pages had kept dry. She shook her head and droplets of water plopped on her lap. Damn, she thought, wiping her face and throat with a tissue. Just her luck. Only an hour earlier, when she'd driven to the home of her client, the sky had been piled with mountains of billowy clouds tinted with the magenta, coral, and gold of another glorious sunset.

After three twists of the ignition key, the car engine gave a rattling cough and sputtered reluctantly into life. Victoria switched on the defogger, but its puny wheeze did little to clear the steamy windshield. For the hundredth time, she reminded herself how badly she needed a new automobile. This clunker was going to die one day soon, and with her luck, a potential house buyer would be her passenger. She would lose not only her car but also the sale she needed to buy a better one. An endless no-win situation. Sighing, she wiped enough of the glass to see where she was going, then joined the line of traffic inching along Okeechobee Boulevard.

Fifteen minutes later, she parked in front of her West Palm Beach condo. Lightning, accompanied by ear-splitting thunder, still flashed through the slate-gray sky. Her hand on the car door handle, Victoria hesitated a moment before pushing it open. The rain immediately drenched her. Wet anyway, she took a deep breath then jumped out and sprinted to her unit, trying to hurdle puddles but more often splashing into them.

As she juggled with the door key, the strap of her old purse caught on the knob and split. The purse upended and toppled down the stairs like a Slinky, tumbling the contents into puddles and under bushes. Tears of frustration and self-pity blurred her vision while she scrambled to reclaim her belongings.

When she finally squished into the bathroom, she was more than simply wet. Mud coated her knees. Her shredded panty hose stuck to her legs like wet gauze. Her hair was the source of a waterfall that streamed down her back and over her face. And she felt more miserable than any woman deserved.

By the time she had showered and wrapped herself in a bright flower covered cotton robe, the drumming on the roof had slackened into a light thumping and the thunder sounded like a distant mumble. Her feet bare, Victoria pattered out to the screened terrace. The thick evening air filled her nostrils with the musty scent of rain-moistened earth. She breathed deeply, savoring the sweetness of night-blooming jasmine and the myriad other flowers that grew in the common area behind the row of condominiums.

Pulling the wrapper tighter around her, she sat in a lounge chair and closed her eyes. The serenade of the frogs and crickets was a balm to her troubled soul.

Didn't it just figure, she sighed. As soon as she was safely out of the rain, it stopped. The story of her life lately. Happiness eluded her by minutes.

Just last week she'd found a client interested in buying a house, only to learn that it had been sold the day before. Just last month she'd thought she had a boyfriend, only to learn he planned to marry someone else—a chic blonde from upscale Palm Beach whose father could afford to invest in Eddie's business scheme. Just last year she was well on her way to proving to her doubtful parents and scornful brother and sister that she could succeed as a real estate agent, only to have the market slump.

She opened her eyes. Clouds, backlit by the rising moon, swirled and eddied as they drifted away. One massive cloud parted like the Red Sea, and a lone star twinkled against the black sky.

"Star light, star bright, first star I see to-night," she intoned that childhood incantation, "I wish. . . ." She wished for so much.

For enough money to buy whatever she needed, with a little left over for trifles.

For success and everything that went with it.

For her family to take her career seriously.

For a man to love who loved her in return.

For happiness.

She took a deep breath and whispered, "I wish someone would buy the Palmworth mansion so that I'll earn that tremendous commission."

Chapter One

"Your exclusive on that white elephant in Palm Beach runs out this week, doesn't it?" Wendy Neff hitched her slender hip onto the edge of Victoria's desk.

Victoria sensed her colleague's smugness, her happiness that Victoria Gordon had failed once again. Reluctant to let the other woman see that her barb had found its mark, she forced a smile.

"Yes." She opened her briefcase and riffled through the papers inside, hoping Wendy would take the hint and go away. "It expires day after tomorrow."

Wendy tilted her head, and with a red acrylic nail traced the length of her long blond hair, then coiled a wave around her finger. "Too bad. You sure spent a lot of time and money promoting that monstrosity."

Anger coursed along Victoria's spine and zipped to the tips of her clear-polished fingernails. She bit back a retort. What would be accomplished by al-

11

lowing Wendy to provoke her. If anything, she'd probably be labeled a troublemaker and asked to leave the real estate agency, in keeping with the downward spiral her life seemed to be taking these days.

She was flashing a dark look at her nemesis when she noticed two men across the room. Matt Claussen, a financial advisor who represented a few of the other, money-earning real estate agents, stood up and gave her a friendly smile as he headed toward the front door. Tall, dark, and handsome, with eyes as blue as the Florida sky, his visits to the agency made the women twitter like a flock of starlings. Except Victoria.

It was the other man who attracted her. Dain Becker, another realtor, grinned at Wendy and lowered one eyelid over sexy green eyes. Victoria turned away, disappointed that he'd winked at Wendy and not her. Nevertheless, her heart skipped a beat while a flurry of excitement jiggled up her spine just at the sight of him.

Even when she'd been involved with Eddie, she hadn't been immune to Dain's attractions. Sure she knew he turned on the charm like a light switch. Sure he never once indicated he had a special interest in her. Still, her body reacted as if it belonged to a giddy teenager instead of a mature 28-year-old businesswoman.

She watched the door swing shut behind Matt's broad back. And encouraged by the memory of his smile, she looked Wendy in the eye and spoke, enunciating every word. "First of all, the house is not a monstrosity. It's just very big—too big for most people. But the grounds are lush and gorgeous. And the seclusion makes it perfect for a celebrity with a lot of money and a need for privacy. That's why I advertised in magazines and newspapers like *Variety* that are read by entertainment and sports figures. If it had sold, my investment would have repaid itself handsomely."

Handsomely, indeed, she thought. The regular realtor's six percent commission plus a five percent bonus on every dollar above the three-million-dollar minimum the seller had set. Obviously, it was a pie-in-the-sky dream. That house wasn't going to sell. As lovely as it was, no one was interested in a house that had more rooms than some hotels, larger and lusher grounds than some parks.

Wendy shook her head as if in commiseration. To Victoria's distrustful eyes, her grimace looked more like a repressed smile than the frown she was trying to convey. "But it didn't sell."

Victoria slammed the briefcase shut and grasped the handle so tight that her knuckles blanched. She strode the length of the office, wrenched the door open, and stomped out, calling over her shoulder, "There are still two days left!"

She plowed into a wall of flesh and hard muscle. Her breasts, stomach, and thighs, the points of impact, felt as if they'd been caressed. Her lungs emptied with a whoosh. Struggling for breath, she inhaled a masculine, lemon-lime scent.

Matt Claussen.

Without realizing it, she'd come to associate that

13

aroma with the man. She looked up, and her gaze locked with his sky-blue eyes. Then he smiled, and a dimple appeared in his left cheek, gentling his serious, businesslike demeanor.

His strong hands grasped her arms and kept her from ricocheting backward. Heat from those hands burned right through the fabric of her jacket to the skin beneath and left a sensitized imprint of each of his fingers.

"Matt!" Victoria stepped back, patting the tight chignon perched at the base of her hairline. "I'm sorry. I didn't hurt you, did I? I thought you left."

Reluctantly, because it was the first time he'd ever touched her, Matt loosened his hold. Even through her clothing, his fingers had felt the delicacy of her frame, the warmth of her skin. He wanted to touch her cheek, just to see if her complexion was as soft as it looked. "No you didn't hurt me," he said, "and no I didn't leave. Just had to get something from my car."

He watched the rise and fall of her chest as she struggled for air. Sure, she'd been rushing out of the office like rabbit chased by a wolf, but unless she was terribly out of shape, that wasn't reason enough for her breathlessness.

"Are you okay?" he asked.

"Just fine." Her voice held more than a trace of bitterness.

Matt wondered what had happened in the few minutes since he'd gone out to the parking lot. Earlier, while discussing business with Dain Becker, he'd noted that Victoria and Wendy Neff seemed to

14

be locking horns. That argument must have ended badly.

"Where were you going in such a hurry?"

"Home. I have work to do and thought I'd get more accomplished there. It's much quieter than the office." She started to walk away. "See ya."

He took her arm in a feather-light grip. After she'd turned down his last casual invitation to lunch, he'd accepted that she wasn't interested and vowed not to ask her again. But now, encouraged by her reaction to their unsettling encounter, he decided to ask one last time. "Hold on a minute."

She arched an eyebrow.

"Since you don't have any appointments, why don't I take you to lunch? My business with Becker is just about wrapped up."

"No thanks." Victoria appreciated the accountant's friendly offer but wasn't in the mood for bantering across a restaurant table. "I really have a lot of work."

All she needed to do to free herself from his grasp was to move her arm. Not sure that she wanted to be released from the curious heat he still radiated, she hesitated. Then she regained her common sense, said "Good-bye," and hurried to the parking lot.

Her car, when new, had been impressively plush, perfect for driving clients to see houses. Now, old and needing repairs she couldn't afford, it sweltered in the sun beside Wendy's brand-new red sports car. She was tempted to kick one of those shiny black tires, but reminded herself she was an adult, a mature professional, and turned her back on the offending vehicle.

When she opened the door of her car, heat struck her as if she'd walked into a furnace. Reluctantly, she got in and, with a crank almost too hot to touch, rolled down the windows. After several tries, the engine coughed, shuddered, and held, and she backed out.

Stopped at a traffic light, she wondered why Wendy always got to her. She felt like kicking herself. Every time she reacted to that witch's sniping, she played right into her hands. But she knew why. She was frustrated, unhappy, and broke, and Wendy took pleasure in rubbing her nose in her failures. It was almost as if the woman were jealous—of what, she couldn't imagine. Wendy had everything: chic, professional success, popularity. None of which could remotely describe her, Victoria.

She knew she wasn't as pretty as the other realtor, but she also knew she was smarter. Knew she deserved at least as much success.

An inner voice asked, *If I'm so smart, why did I list that house in Palm Beach when so many others had tried to sell it and failed?* Because, she answered herself, she was born with an optimistic spirit that took beating after beating without giving in.

She looked up at the sky and saw the color of Matt's eyes in the incredible blue. What had happened to her back there when they collided? The man had been coming into the office for about a

16

year. Always friendly, he frequently invited her to come along when he and the others went to lunch or for a drink after work—even mentioned one of those summer pop concerts in the park—invitations she'd never taken seriously or accepted. She had never physically reacted to him before, either. Actually, now that she thought about it, they'd never touched before. Not even a handshake. It was Dain who always made the skin on her spine tingle.

The light turned to green, and a car behind her honked. Quickly stepping on the accelerator, she shrugged off her reaction to Matt as some sort of shock caused by the impact of their collision. That was all. She wasn't going to give it another thought.

The phone was ringing when she unlocked the door of her condo. She ran across the tiled entry and caught the phone on the fourth ring, before the answering machine could click in.

"Hello?"

"Is this Victoria Gordon?"

"Yes." She took off her simple gold-tone hoop earring and slipped out of her low-heeled white pumps.

"My name is William Hammond. I represent Alice Benning. She asked me to look at that property in Palm Beach you advertised."

"The talk show hostess?"

Victoria's heart lurched.

Benning was currently gliding on a wave of popularity just a notch below Oprah and Sally. A sale to her would represent much more than the very generous commission. Doors to influential contacts, normally closed to people like her, would be flung open. She'd be on her way! Excitement zigzagged through her like lightning.

"Yes. That's right," the man replied. "When can you show me the house? She trusts my judgment implicitly. I'll know if it's worth the six million dollar asking price."

Someone in the office must be pulling a prank, Victoria thought. But though she listened closely, the voice wasn't familiar, nor did it sound disguised. She decided to treat the call as authentic on the off-chance it was.

"Today is fine," she said. "Whenever it's convenient for you."

"I'm in Miami. I could drive up to Palm Beach this afternoon. Would five o'clock be okay?"

"Absolutely. My office is—"

"Why don't we just meet in Palm Beach," he suggested. "Wouldn't that be closer? I'll have a long enough drive as it is."

"Yes. Of course. No problem."

After arranging where to meet, she hung up. If her so-called friends were tricking her, she'd be so angry, she'd . . .

Enough of that negative attitude, she admonished herself. Today, Victoria Gordon was going to sell one of the most expensive houses in Palm Beach to one of the most popular talk show hosts on television. Her nerve endings still tingling, she forced herself to believe that something good was finally going to happen to her.

Without conscious thought, she reached for the

phone, wanting, needing to share her excitement with someone. She had punched in the first four digits of Eddie's number before remembering that he wouldn't care. That he was on his honeymoon with the beautiful blond heiress he'd met at the polo club. That he was lost to her forever. And truth to tell, she didn't give a damn.

Eddie hadn't been much of a boyfriend, dropping in when he had nothing else to do, bringing video tapes rather than taking her to a movie theater. When they went out to eat, it was usually for a pizza, and more often than not, she paid. But even worse, he gave her no emotional support. He rarely listened when she wanted to vent her frustrations over her stagnant career or her unhappiness with her family's lack of understanding. The heiress, she knew, had done her a favor by releasing her from a dead-end, boring relationship that she hadn't had the energy to get out of herself.

A tear of self-pity trickled down her cheek. If all went well, this would be the happiest day of her life. Yet she had no one to share it with.

Briefly, she thought of calling her parents back in Minnesota, but they wouldn't understand her excitement. She could almost hear her mother saying, "That's nice, dear, but when are you going to give up all this career nonsense and settle down with some nice young man?"

Matt Claussen flashed through her mind. But she hardly knew him and doubted if she ever would.

Impatiently, she brushed away the tear and straightened her spine. Today she was going to attain her dreams of success and wealth. If she wanted to make a good impression on Mr. Hammond, she'd better stop wasting time feeling sorry for herself and get ready to meet him.

Later, wrapped in a plush bath sheet, her light brown hair shower-wet against her naked back, she surveyed the dark suits and dresses that hung in her closet like shadowy sentinels to her drab, prosaic life. Finally, she chose a white silk blouse to wear beneath a classic black suit.

At five sharp, William Hammond, a short balding middle-aged man who oozed success, from his Italian leather shoes to his Armani suit and Vuarnet sunglasses, pulled into the Palm Beach parking lot Victoria had designated as their meeting place. Looking down his beaky nose at her ancient car, he offered to drive. He didn't have to offer twice. The humidity was higher than the temperature, and Victoria's air conditioning balked when the mercury rose above sixty degrees. Wiping her brow when he looked the other way, she swallowed her pride, slid gratefully into his rented Mercedes, and directed him to Ocean Boulevard.

After they had glided past a series of stucco walls and tall hedges that shut out the world from Palm Beach's finest homes, she directed Hammond to turn onto a driveway between wrought iron gates.

"Normally these gates are kept locked. But I called the owner, and he left them open for us."

Hammond nodded and guided the car along the circular driveway. He stopped beneath the bougainvillea-draped portico. As he got out, he swept a casual glance over the Spanish-style house with its red tiled roof and dazzling white stucco walls.

At the massive front door, Victoria took the key from the lockbox and let them in. Though she had visited the house many times, she was still awed by it. Terra-cotta floors. Vaulted ceilings. Marble hallways. The kitchen was newly remodeled and equipped with all the latest equipment and gadgetry. Each wall of the library was lined with floor-to-ceiling bookshelves. A lifetime's worth of reading filled the room, and the sitting area in front of the leaded windows enticed the reader to curl up and drift into other worlds.

After a thorough tour of the first floor, where Hammond poked his head into each closet, turned on every one of the golden faucets, and paced out the length of the ballroom-sized salon, Victoria led him up the sweeping staircase to the second floor.

"Notice the mahogany of the balustrade matches the baseboards and moldings. That elaborate motif is repeated throughout the house."

Hammond traced a carved rose on the newel post with his finger but said not a word. Although she could usually gauge a buyer's interest, this man had her stymied. He was as cool as a ski slope in January. All she could do was continue with the walkthrough and hope for the best.

On the second floor, Benning's representative checked out each bedroom, bath, and closet. Without comment, he looked through windows at the ocean view at the front of the house. He asked her to turn on the whirlpool tub in the master suite.

"Miss Benning can relax in the tub and watch the world go by through that window," Victoria suggested.

"If Miss Benning was content to watch the world go by, she wouldn't be where she is today."

"Yes, of course." Victoria cleared her throat, feeling properly chastised. "Let me show you the gardens."

She escorted Hammond back down the staircase and into a dining room large enough to accommodate a table that could seat two dozen or more. French doors led to a terrace beneath Moorish arches.

"Let's go out here," she suggested.

They meandered through the more than two acres of lawns and gardens, over a stone and shell path to the gazebo, then to a small pond overflowing with pink water lilies.

"The owner tried to keep koi in the pond," she explained, "but the herons kept eating them. So he settled for flowers instead. Isn't it gorgeous?"

"Mmm," Hammond said distractedly, looking beyond the pond toward the guest house. "Gorgeous."

Victoria sensed the showing wasn't going well. She didn't have Hammond's attention. Whenever she pointed out a particularly spectacular asset of the house, his attention was on something else.

He wasn't going to recommend buying the house. Her life wasn't going to change. She was going to be stuck in the same awful rut until she finally gave up and crawled back to Minnesota, a reluctant lamb returning to the fold. She saw him head toward the kidney-shaped pool and scurried after him. At least he was still looking around and hadn't suggested they leave.

"There are two tennis courts." She pointed beyond a thick lawn toward an area enclosed by a chain-link fence. "Lighted, of course."

"Yes. They would have to be. Your ad indicated several citrus trees. Coming from a cold climate, Ms Benning considers them exotic and wanted to be assured the trees you mentioned were actually productive."

"This way." As Victoria spoke, Hammond fell into step beside her until they came to the perimeter of the small grove. "As you can see, there are lemon, orange, and grapefruit trees. All with lots of fruit. When the trees are in bloom, the whole area smells divine."

"I'm sure it does." He scowled at the trees as if they were poison oak.

Victoria's heart went down for the third time.

Without much hope, she started back to the house but paused beneath the shade of a royal poinciana tree. Just a few flaming red blossoms clung to its spreading branches. "This tree is almost finished flowering now, but when it's in full bloom, it's a magnificent sight."

"I'm sure it is."

Entering the house through the kitchen door, Victoria said, "It's a beautiful home." She believed every word but doubted if Hammond agreed.

Someone else would have to sell the house, because her final hope didn't like it at all.

"Ms Benning will take it," Hammond said with as much enthusiasm as a customer buying a loaf of bread.

"What?" Victoria was sure she had misheard him.

"We'll have to negotiate the details, of course. But Ms Benning would like to take possession as soon as possible."

Victoria's heart leaped.

She swallowed hard. "I'm sure that can be arranged. The current owner is very agreeable." She didn't tell him that the current owner was so anxious to get out that he'd offered her a bonus if she sold the place.

"Since time is of the essence, can we discuss this right here?" Hammond asked. "Is the owner on the premises?"

"No. He mentioned that he was going out to dinner. But I'm sure he won't mind if we use his office. Right this way."

Twenty-four hours after Victoria showed Alice Benning's representative the "white elephant" in Palm Beach, he brought a certified check into the escrow office. It was one of the fastest property sales in Florida history.

Twenty-four hours after she showed William Hammond the "white elephant" in Palm Beach, Victoria pocketed a commission check for

$315,000. In her estimation, she was a very rich woman.

The day the deed to the mansion was transferred to its new owner, Victoria practically floated into the real estate office, her feet feeling as if they were several inches off the ground. All heads swiveled her way, but she pretended not to notice, pretended to be as cool as a mint julep, pretended her heart was beating normally, not dancing a fandango against her ribs.

The first person to greet her was Irene, the middle-aged receptionist. "I made sure everyone heard your good news." Irene's embrace, warm and sincere, reminded Victoria she did have friends who cared about her.

Dain came up, elbowed Irene aside, and crushed Victoria in a bear hug that whooshed the air from her lungs.

"I'm so happy for you," he whispered in her ear.

Delicious chills flickered up her spine. "Thanks, Dain." To her surprise, and delight, he kept his arm wrapped possessively around her waist.

After graciously accepting congratulations from everyone, even a reluctant Wendy, Victoria, her voice filled with pride, said: "Come outside. I want to show you my new car. I paid cash for it."

On her way to work, she had stopped at an automobile showroom and traded in her old clunker for a new BMW that was brighter, redder, and more luxurious than Wendy's. As she sat behind the wheel, breathing in that magical new-car smell, she felt as if her heart would burst with happiness. "Mine," she whispered. "I earned it. All by myself."

Then in a boutique on Worth Avenue in Palm Beach, she had tried on a variety of dresses before choosing a blue silk shirtwaist that draped from her slender waist in graceful folds. Elegantly understated, it cost more than she'd earned the previous month. So what, she'd thought, as she admired herself in the dressing room mirror, she could afford it.

Now, with Dain's arm around her waist, she led her colleagues out to ooh and aah over her new automobile. Wendy, she noted with a tinge of disappointment, stayed behind to answer the phones.

"Are you still going to work here?" Mary Vandekker asked.

"Yes, of course. For a while, anyway. Until I'm ready to go off on my own."

"Maybe we could open an office together," Dain crooned.

Goose bumps followed their usual path along her spine. When she smiled at him, his fingers dug into her flesh slightly, making her feel a bit uncomfortable yet oddly exhilarated.

Wendy came out of the office and shouted, "Dain! You have a phone call."

"Sorry, darling. I'd better take that." Dain slowly eased his arm from her waist. "Let's do lunch — soon."

Another parade of goose bumps.

The others followed Dain into the building, but Irene hung back, linking arms with Victoria.

Victoria could see Wendy staring through the glass door. "What is with that woman?" she wondered aloud.

"She's jealous," Irene declared.

"Jealous? Of what?"

"Take a really good look in the mirror sometime. You're the only woman in the office who's not only prettier than she is but who's also her business equal."

"Oh, come on, Irene. You have an overactive imagination."

The receptionist shrugged and changed the subject. "That's a very pretty car."

"Thanks."

"And dress."

"I'm glad you like it." Her back straightened with pride. She'd done it all herself and proved the skeptics back in Minnesota wrong. She could be a successful career woman. "It cost a small fortune."

"I thought as much. Victoria, do you think it's wise to spend all that money so quickly?"

"Why not? I earned it. No one's going to take it away from me."

Irene persisted. "Don't you think you ought to call Matt Claussen?"

"What for?"

"For advice."

Resentment displaced pride. What gave Irene the right to tell her what to do—to imply that she was incapable of handling her own financial affairs? She'd had enough of that from her parents and siblings. "I don't need advice. I have everything I want."

"If you want to keep the money . . ." the receptionist glanced pointedly toward the door Dain had used a few minutes earlier. ". . . you'd better call Matt." Either oblivious to Victoria's change of mood, or indifferent to it, Irene kept talking. "First of all, there's the taxes. Uncle Sam is going to get a big chunk of that money."

"Well . . . ," Victoria hedged, "I know that. But there's an awful lot to spend." Although she wouldn't admit it to Irene, Victoria knew she would have to hire a good accountant to handle her tax returns.

"Let me get Matt on the phone for you. I've heard really good things about him. My folks used his financial management service when they retired, and they've been very pleased. At least listen to what the man has to say."

Victoria nodded, her feet finally nearing the ground. "Okay. Call him. And thanks."

"You're welcome, honey. Will you make the call from your desk? Or on that shiny new car phone?"

Victoria laughed. "At my desk."

A few minutes later, the receiver pressed to her ear, she heard Matt say, "So you sold the old Palmworth mansion?"

"Sure did. To Alice Benning."

"Your commission must have been astronomical."

"It was." She named the six-figure amount she still couldn't believe she'd earned from just one sale.

He whistled — a long drawn-out, high-pitched note.

"Irene suggested that I talk to you about it," Victoria said.

"Smart woman. Don't spend a penny until we've worked out a plan."

"Actually, I already have bought a couple of things." She transferred the phone to her other ear, thinking "a couple of things" was a bit of an understatement.

"Well, don't buy anything else. The more you invest, the bigger your income will be. And you have to allow for taxes." He paused then asked, "Are you free for lunch today?"

She looked longingly at Dain who was still on the phone. "I suppose so." Dain had said lunch soon, not specifically today. So, unfortunately, she was free.

"The Pink Shrimp Cafe on Okeechobee Boulevard? One o'clock?"

"Okay," Victoria said, almost reluctantly. "I'll be there."

"I'll call ahead for reservations."

As she hung up, she hoped Matt wouldn't want to tie up all her assets in investments. For too many years she'd pinched pennies. Now she felt like a bird let out of its cage for the first time. A little frightened, a little overwhelmed. But most of all, free.

Chapter Two

Seated at a table in the Pink Shrimp Cafe, his chair facing the door, Matt waited for Victoria. When he saw her come in, he got to his feet and watched her approach.

He admired the way the silky material of her dress clung to her hips and insinuated itself across her thighs, creating tantalizing shadows and light with each step she took. As she drew closer, he saw that the blue of the dress flattered her golden skin. Too bad the hemline was so long. One of those minis would have been better. He grinned. He sure would like to see more of her legs. The trim ankles and curvaceous calves he glimpsed below the swirling fabric offered a promise that sent his hormone level soaring.

"Hi," she said.

Matt held her chair and pushed it in after she sat down. Unable to resist the urge to touch her, he skimmed his hand across her back. As he'd suspected, it felt warm and silky, just as he knew her bare skin would feel, if ever he had the chance to touch it. He cleared his throat before he could speak.

"Congratulations." He sat down again.

"Thanks." She flashed a hundred kilowatt smile.

"I ordered champagne."

"Well, thanks again." The sparkle in her eyes winked like stars. "That was very kind of you."

Her brightness dazzled him. The contrast between her usual drab self and the woman sitting across from him was like a penlight to a beacon. "Your success calls for a celebration."

"I couldn't agree more." She leaned back and gave a smug grin that said she'd grasped the brass ring and intended never to let go.

He took the champagne from the ice-filled bucket beside him and filled two fluted glasses. He raised his. "To continued success. It couldn't have happened to a more deserving woman."

She bobbed her head in thanks and took a generous sip. "Mmmm. This is good stuff. Thanks—again."

Her happiness was thanks enough. In the year or so he'd known her, he could't remember one time when her smile had reached her eyes and made them sparkle as they did now. He was gratified that his gesture of ordering champagne had added to her happiness. He didn't want to see the smile fade, didn't want the fragile, special moment to end.

He said, "Why don't we eat before we get down to business."

"Sounds good." She picked up her menu. When

the waitress arrived, pen and pad in hand, Victoria ordered a shrimp Louis salad.

While she nibbled on a bread stick, she said, "I guess I've known you for about, what . . . ?" She shrugged. "A year? And I don't know a thing about you."

"You should have used my financial services."

She gave a dry laugh. "I should have needed your financial services. You're from California, aren't you?"

"Yup. I moved here a couple of years ago from Los Angeles."

"How come? I thought L.A. was the epitome of . . . something or other."

"It is. I worked for a top rated firm there. Saved every penny I could because I wanted to go out on my own. Finally, when I had enough money put aside, I quit. But there's no room in L.A. for another financial advisor—good as I am."

While she smiled at his little joke, he looked inward, remembering the competition among the executives of the firm. Arriving earlier and earlier, staying later and later, until they were so exhausted their work began to suffer. And in the end, when it came to the next promotion, some outsider was hired. But when it came to layoffs, whole departments were swept away, the hard-working executives included. He was one of the so-called lucky ones who'd kept his job. But next time, who knew? And there'd always be a next time.

He picked up the thread of his story. "So I checked out several areas of the country where

I thought I might like to live. Then studied the markets. And here I am."

"Fortunately for me." Victoria lifted her glass, tilted it toward him, then took another sip.

Matt studied her heart-shaped face, hoping to find a hidden meaning behind her statement. Despite the physical stirrings he'd felt earlier — and was still feeling — he didn't forget this was a business meeting, much as he wished he could. So he didn't misinterpret her words.

"I'm glad you think so," he said. "When we first spoke, I had the impression you were consulting me under duress."

"Oh no. On the contrary. I need your advice. Ultimately, if — when — I sell some other houses and have enough seed money, I'd like to open my own office. When the time comes, I want you to help me set it up. And I need someone to help me with the IRS. And—"

"What you want, Victoria," he cut in, "is an accountant. I'm a financial advisor. I'll gladly do all those other things for you because I'm a licensed CPA, but basically, if you retain my services, my job will be to guide your investments."

"Oh? I haven't thought that about that."

"Which is exactly why you need me."

Victoria waited until the waitress placed her shrimp Louis in front of her before responding. "I don't want to tie up my money. I want to be . . . what's the term? Liquid?"

"You can be liquid and still well invested," Matt

said, leaning forward slightly, linking his gaze to hers.

She blinked against the dazzle in his eyes and fought his magnetism.

"I have some ideas to discuss with you," he continued. "Why don't we go back to my office after lunch? It's not far from here. And we can talk without interruptions. Let's just enjoy lunch now."

With a slight toss of her head, Victoria said, "Sure."

She'd been in business long enough to know when someone wanted something from her. And Matt Claussen stood to earn a big commission off her own big commission. The more she invested with him, the more money he'd make. And the less money she'd have to spend on herself and her dreams. Her eyes narrowed.

"What's the matter?" he asked.

"Nothing. I'm not sure if I want to invest my money."

"What do you want to do with it?"

"Spend it." Her penny-pinching days were over.

"That's the point of investing. You'll have the interest to spend while the principal's earning more money. If you spend the principal, before you know it, it's all gone." Placing his hands on the table, he turned his palms up as if eliciting her trust. "When I lay out the details of my plans for you, I think it'll make more sense."

Then, like putting a period at the end of a sentence, he dropped a dab of sour cream on his baked potato, closing the topic. "I understand you started working in the real estate office about four years ago?"

"That's right." She allowed him to steer the conversation away from his business and back to hers. "Who told you?"

"Becker."

Victoria smiled. So Dain had been talking about her. Good. It meant she was on his mind.

"After I graduated from Miami U, I went home to Minneapolis," she said. "I spent two miserable years fighting the freezing winters. Guess my blood thinned from living in this warm climate. Just couldn't take the cold anymore." She popped a forkful of her salad into her mouth, the red sauce tangy on her tongue, the lettuce fresh and crisp.

"I was a sales executive at a manufacturing firm," she said. Then, like a child taking comfort from its security blanket, she ran a hand over her severe hairstyle, enjoying its sleek smoothness. "But I got tired of my job." And tired of the games that stopped just short of sexual harassment. Tired of siblings who still thought of her as a kid and couldn't pass up any opportunity to ridicule her dreams. Tired of parents who thought she should marry the boy next door and give them grandchildren. A family that meant well but didn't take her desire for a career seriously. Without their moral support, there had been nothing to keep her in Minnesota.

"So I came back to Florida, got my real estate license, then hooked up with the Realty Consortium. Until the last few months I was doing well enough to think the time had come to open my own agency. Then the market slumped."

As she spoke, his eyes studied her face. He listened to her intently, seeming to hang onto every word as if it were the Dow Jones Report. Because his interest appeared so genuine, she had an overwhelming desire to tell him about her dream—a secret she hadn't even shared with Eddie, it was so close to her heart.

She put her fork down, looked at the couple at the next table, and lowered her voice. "In addition to opening my own real estate brokerage company, I want to franchise eventually. Maybe even get into developing. Now that I have this money, I can think about it seriously." She held her breath, waiting for him to laugh at her.

Instead, Matt touched her hand lightly, fleetingly, but with a finger hot as flame. "That's a wonderful dream. It'll come true—one day. Unfortunately, real estate sales are down just about everywhere right now. You'd be better off waiting until the market picks up a little. It will, you know."

Disappointed that he hadn't embraced her idea as enthusiastically as she'd hoped, yet relieved he hadn't made fun of her dreams, Victoria lowered her eyes and let the air out of her lungs slowly. She studied the back of her hand. The spot he'd touched still tingled.

She raised her gaze to regard him directly and openly. At least he was taking her seriously. A coil of tension tightened inside her when she saw the raw yearning deep in his eyes. Then he blinked, and his expression was once again bland and friendly. Although she must have imagined his emotion, her own feelings were jumbled and confused. Was there something more to his interest than business?

After struggling to regain the thread of the conversation, she forced herself to say, "I know the market will turn around. But I'm not sure if I want to wait. This might actually be a good time. While the market's depressed, I'll be able to get concessions on office rent. Since I'm not that busy anyway, I'd have plenty of time to set things up."

"You make a valid point." He finished the last of his blackened red snapper and wiped his lips with his napkin. "I blocked off some time for you this afternoon. We could discuss it then. How about it?"

Why was he pressuring her? Obviously, she'd been misinterpreting his reactions, and hers as well. His apparent interest in her was purely professional.

She said, "Not this afternoon. I'm seeing a client. After word got out about my sale, I received several calls from people who want me to list their homes. Maybe I'll specialize in the hard-to-sell." She nodded. "That's an idea. Yeah. That's what I'm going to do. What do you think?" Enthusiasm for the new concept caught her imagination, and again she waited breathlessly for his approval.

"Sounds good," he said. "But you'd better sell the houses, or you'll go broke — unless you have a solid portfolio of investments to keep you going — to back you up."

"Please don't pressure me, Matt." Her voice was chilly. "I'll have to think about it."

He put his hands up defensively. "Okay. Just let me know when you decide."

The waitress came to the table holding a tray laden with calorie-filled pastries, including Black Forest cake, rum babas and Sacher torte. "How about dessert? The chef bakes an excellent Key lime pie."

Shaking her head, Victoria studied the contents of the tray. "Couldn't eat another bite."

"We could share a piece," Matt suggested.

"We-el." She grinned. "I suppose I could find the room for a little bit."

"Good." He nodded to the waitress, then turned back to Victoria. "Coffee?"

"Sure."

He held up two fingers.

"Coming right up." The waitress scribbled in her pad, then left them.

When the pie came a few minutes later, Victoria dug in just as Matt, too, put his fork into the creamy light green custard. The forks clicked like swords, and they laughed.

He pulled his away. "You first."

"Thanks." She cut off the pointed end of the slice and raised it to her lips.

As he took his own piece, he watched the tips of her fork disappear between her lips. Her tongue darted out to catch a crumb. He wanted to lean over and flick his tongue on hers. Patience, he counseled himself. He didn't want to scare her away by moving too fast.

He savored the tang of lime in his own mouth and knew how she'd taste. Clean and sweet. If he dropped his fork, would she share hers? Would she feed him? He put his fork down. The less he ate, the more she would have. And he wanted to watch her enjoy the pie, although each time her tongue licked her lips, his body tightened with need. Was there a man in her life? Someone who was kissing those tempting lips? He'd seethe with jealousy if there was. But he had to know.

When she'd mashed up the last of the crumbs with her fork and eaten them, Matt asked, "Is there anyone special in your life?"

Victoria's eyes widened at the question. She rocked her fork back and forth while trying to decide whether or not to answer him. And if she did, what should her response be? For a moment she thought of Dain, but he wasn't in her life. While Matt waited for her answer, he took a swallow of coffee. His eyes never left her face.

"No," she said. "No one." Eddie was history, not even worth mentioning. "How about you?"

If he could ask personal questions, so could she. Besides, she really wanted to know. Not for herself, of course. But she could tell Mary back at the office. She'd been wondering.

He hesitated for a moment as if he, too, were debating how much of his personal life to reveal. "Nope," he said, his grin creating that dimple in his left cheek. "I left a string of broken hearts in California, of course." His eyes sparkled.

"Of course," she said, chuckling. Mary would be pleased.

He laughed with her, then became serious. "But there's no one here."

"Lonely?"

"No. Not really. I've been too busy. Starting a new business is very time-consuming."

For a fleeting moment, Victoria wondered what it would be like if Matt wasn't too busy, and she was the woman he chose to spend his time with. Silly goose, she called herself. Besides, she wasn't interested in him. If she wanted any man, which she didn't, her choice would be Dain Becker.

By the time they were lingering over their coffee, Victoria felt less wary of Matt, more at ease. Yet the almost chemical reaction wavered between them like a heat mirage.

They were discussing their favorite movies when Matt said, "I hear that new comedy playing at the triplex is very good. Have you seen it?"

"Nope. I don't get to the movies much. I usually wait till they come out on video." As she said it, she realized it had been more than three months since she'd been in a movie theater.

"Why is that?"

Victoria shrugged. Since her relationship with Eddie had ended, she rarely went out. And she hadn't gotten out that much even when she was dating him. But that information was none of Matt's business.

"I'd really like to see that film," he said. "Why don't we catch it tomorrow evening?"

Victoria arched one well shaped eyebrow. Was he asking her for a date? His manner casual, his blue gaze intent on her face, he sipped his coffee and waited. Something in that gaze reached into her heart. Her skin prickled. She looked away.

Why would he want to take her to the movies? To soft-sell her into letting him invest her money? Because he felt as if he'd been backed into a corner and had to ask her? Whatever his motives, men like Matt Claussen didn't date women like Victoria Gordon. Handsome as he was, she knew he could have any girl he wanted. He certainly didn't want plain, conservative Victoria. Feeling wistful, wondering what she'd be missing, she sat a little straighter and let him off the hook.

"No thanks. I've . . . I've got an appointment — to show a house."

He couldn't argue with that excuse, nor would he put himself in the position of being turned down again. But he wasn't going to give up. Tomorrow was another day. "Okay." He shrugged and pushed back his chair. "Are you finished with your coffee?"

Was that a sigh of relief she'd heard?

"Um hum," she said. "Thanks for the lunch. It was delicious."

"My pleasure. I'll be in touch."

At his last words, the flutterings that had been tickling her insides since his fingers accidentally grazed her back vanished like a puff of smoke, replacing titillation with irritation. Sure he'd be in touch, but not because he was interested in her as a

41

woman. And why should he be? The only attractive thing about her was her money. So when he did contact her again, he'd pressure her to invest that hard earned money — with him.

They walked to the parking lot together, his arm barely brushing her elbow. Slight though it was, that touch made every nerve ending acutely aware of him.

Holding her car door while she got in, he said, "This is a beauty. Bet it set you back a good chunk of your commission."

"Sure did. It's an *investment*." She emphasized the last word. "Clients in the financial bracket I intend to attract will be impressed with the car. It screams success. Besides, isn't it tax deductible since it's a business expense?"

"A portion is deductible. Yeah."

"Well, then, be happy for me."

"I am, I just don't want you to spend all your money. Don't forget your dreams for the future." He stepped back.

The engine started with a purr, music to ears that were attuned to a choked grinding. She backed out, then looked in the rear-view mirror. Matt stood where she'd left him, watching her. She waved casually and drove off, luxuriating in the coolness of the air that wafted through the vents.

She deserved this car. She'd earned it. Why should she have to drive that old clunker and suffer in the heat when she could afford the best. Why did Matt Claussen have to make her feel guilty? He wanted a piece of her pie, and because of that, an inner voice cautioned her not to trust him completely.

If she didn't trust him, why had he been able to reach right into her soul and set her afire with just a look. And when his hand had touched hers—whew! It was if he'd held a flamethrower.

She lowered the temperature control. Just remembering her reactions made her warmer.

Matt was the kind of man she used to fantasize about. But long ago she'd given up that particular dream. All the more reason to keep up her guard when he was around. He wanted something from her, and it wasn't the pleasure of her company—or body. It was the green of her money.

Back in the office, Victoria sorted through the mail and messages piled on her desk. Her head bobbed with gratification when she came across an inquiry from another owner anxious to sell his house. If only the inquiries from buyers would come in as quickly. She picked up the phone to return the call and made an appointment for that afternoon.

Later, on the way to the ladies' room, Victoria passed Wendy's desk. Wendy glanced up, then quickly turned away as if even the sight of Victoria was too much to bear. Why? What had she ever done to Wendy to merit such treatment? Could Irene possibly have been right in believing Wendy was jealous. Nah. Impossible. Maybe now she envied the sale of the Palmworth property, but her attitude had been unpleasant for a long time.

Victoria was in a stall when the rest room door

squeaked, followed by the click of high heels on the tile floor.

She heard Wendy say, "I can't believe Victoria's luck. Why her?"

"I don't know." Victoria recognized the other woman's voice as that of Mary Vandecker, another real estate agent. "We all work just as hard as she does."

Instinctively, Victoria flexed her knees and pulled up her feet so the women wouldn't know she was there, although she suspected Wendy was well aware of her presence and was about to steer the conversation in a direction that would hurt her.

"And we're prettier," Wendy said. "I don't know about you, but I owe a lot of my success to my looks. When I turn on the sex appeal, the men eat out of my hand. Victoria's sex appeal is zero."

That particular dart hit the mark, and pain shot through Victoria. But not for one moment did she regret the integrity that had kept her from using her body as a marketing tool. On the contrary, years ago she'd decided that to be taken seriously in the male-dominated world of business, she had to downplay her looks and femininity.

Wendy lowered her voice. "Don't tell anyone I said this, but even in that expensive dress she looks frumpy and older than she really is. That woman needs a whole new wardrobe—she certainly can afford one now."

The trickle of running water was followed by the whisper of paper towel ripping. Victoria fervently hoped that meant the women would soon leave. She was beginning to regret her decision to eavesdrop. Their words stung more than she'd anticipated.

To her dismay, they kept right on gossiping. "And someone to help her pick out her clothes. Maybe I'll volunteer."

Wendy's laugh grated on Victoria's nerves like a barking dog in the middle of the night.

"No wonder she can't hold a man," Mary added. "That creep Eddie dropped her pretty quick—and he wasn't anything to brag about. She doesn't even know how to have fun."

I do, too, Victoria thought. *I just don't have time. And I don't have anyone to have fun with.* A tear gathered in the corner of her eye. She brushed it away before it could drop. These women would never make her cry!

Relentlessly, Mary continued, "I wonder what that guy saw in her in the first place."

There was a pause and Victoria could almost visualize Wendy slashing red lipstick across her catty mouth. "Mouse colored hair pulled back in that fifties' chignon. She looks like her own mother. Her skirts are too long, and her heels are too low and clunky. I wonder if she even owns something in a bright color. She's a drab little mouse."

"A lucky little mouse. What did you think of that car?"

A powder compact snapped shut, then their voices drifted away as they left the room. Slowly, Victoria lowered her feet to the tile floor. Her heart felt as if it were clasped in an ever-tightening vise.

She slid the lock to the left, eased the door open and

peeped out. The powder room was empty. She crossed to the sink and studied her reflection in the mirror.

How dared those women call her a drab mouse. True, her hair was that dull brown that had no sparkle, but what was wrong with the style? It was sophisticated, chosen to make her appear professional and mature. And it was practical, keeping the heavy length off her neck in hot weather.

Peering closer at her reflection, she took an honest look at herself. The chignon wasn't sophisticated; it was outdated and severe. She clicked her purse open and took out a lipstick. The shade was too light, a far cry from Wendy's vivid red. And her cheeks needed more blush. Even with the blue of the dress flattering her complexion, she looked washed out.

Her dress. Was it really too long? She looked down. The hem hit her leg below mid-calf. Other women were wearing skirts that barely covered their thighs, while she was hiding her legs. What was the matter with her? Only twenty-eight and acting like an old lady. Being conservative in her appearance had become so ingrained that she'd let the world pass her by.

She needed to buy new cosmetics, needed a whole new wardrobe. And she needed to have some fun. Wendy thought she was hurting her when she said those awful things. But the cat had tried to claw the mouse once too often.

By the time she left the rest room, Victoria knew exactly what she was going to do.

Chapter Three

"Victoria!" cried Irene. "What have you done to yourself?" The receptionist gaped in wonder.

As Victoria pirouetted, her hair drifted around her shoulders in honey-gold waves, and the skirt of her red silk dress swirled like a bullfighter's cape above her knees.

"Do you like it? I spent yesterday afternoon at Leonardo's Beauty Salon." She fluffed her hair. "And a fashion consultant at the Starlight Boutique is choosing a wardrobe for me. I go back next week for the final selections. Isn't it wonderful?" She didn't wait for Irene's response, but gushed on. "I've even changed my name to Tori. Victoria sounds stodgy. And conservative. Tori is youthful and fun. Actually it's an old new name. Didn't call myself Victoria till after college. Thought it made me sound more mature. Before then I was always Tori." She finally stopped to take a breath.

Irene came around her desk and gave her friend

a hug. "I love it all. You're gorgeous." She glanced into the empty office area. "Wait till the others see you!"

Tori smiled hesitantly, her self-confidence faltering for an instant. "I couldn't wait to show you. You really like it?"

"Yes. I really like it."

Tori's glorious smile was back to place. "Dain in yet?" she asked although it was obvious he wasn't.

Irene wrinkled her nose. "He's never early. You know that. You're first in this morning." The phone rang and Irene reached across her desk to answer it. She waved to Tori as if to say, "I'll talk to you later."

Tori sashayed to her desk, but before she had time to sit down, Irene came over.

"That was my son's school. He got hurt in PE. I've got to go get him."

Tori looked at her with concern. "Nothing serious, I hope."

"It doesn't sound like it, but I'll feel better after I see for myself. Maybe take him to the doctor. Would you cover the phones until I get back? If I'll be more than an hour, I'll let you know."

"No problem. I don't have any appointments till this afternoon. And I'm sure the others will help out."

With an unladylike snort of disbelief, Irene grabbed her purse and left.

Tori settled herself behind Irene's desk, oblivious to the prospectus for a new housing project she'd spread out across it. Chin propped on her hand, she gazed into space, her mind replaying Irene's reaction. She'd been pleased with the changes Tori had made in her appearance, and her friend was one of the few people whose judgment and honesty Tori trusted. Her confidence jumped another notch.

A car pulled into the parking lot, crossing Tori's line of vision. She blinked then shook her head, returning to the present. She peeked at her watch. The others should be coming in any minute. She fluffed her hair, smoothed her skirt. Then she picked up the picture frame which held a photo of Irene's family and checked her lipstick in the distorted reflection she saw on the glass. Looking over the frame, she saw that someone was coming. Her heart jackhammered.

Her head was bent over the glossy catalogue, her hair screening her face, when Dain strolled in.

"Hi, beautiful," he said.

Tori looked up and smiled.

A grin flashed whitely on Dain's handsome, suntanned face. His charm, cranked up to high voltage, was almost tangible. "You're new around here. How come I haven't seen you before? Where have you been all my li—" He leaned closer and squinted into her features. "Victoria?"

Her heart doing happy flip-flops at Dain's reaction, Tori watched, fascinated, while his expression changed rapidly from flirtatious, to shocked, then appreciative. His face was such an open book that she could see when he switched back to flirtatious.

He reached over the desk and rubbed a golden strand of her hair between his fingers. "Lovely. What a surprise."

Did he realize his backhanded compliment was more insult than praise? she wondered. Yet his attentions sent those shivers up her spine. So what if he was a little tactless. He was handsome and sexy. And she needed the attentions of such a man. Her ego had taken quite a beating the day before.

"Stand up," he said. "Let me see the rest of you."

As Tori pirouetted again, teetering slightly on her new three-inch heels, Wendy opened the door. Tori almost twirled into it. Dain grasped her arm to keep her from falling.

"Always have to make a play for the new girls, don't you, Dain?" Wendy asked. "Haven't you heard sexual harassment in the workplace is a no-no? One of these days you're going to be slapped with a lawsuit." She turned to the blonde who had moved into the square of morning light which beamed through the plate-glass window.

Dain declared, "Keep your nasty cracks to yourself. She isn't a new girl. She's Victoria."

But Dain needn't have bothered with introductions, for Wendy looked stunned, her mouth wide with astonishment.

"Better shut your trap or you're going to attract flies," Dain declared. "Or better yet, palmetto bugs."

Ignoring him, Wendy said, "Victoria? Is it really you?"

Tori relished the moment, wishing it would never end. The thrill of selling that house and earning that huge commission was almost topped by the satisfaction from Wendy's reaction. This single moment avenged all the hurtful, biting remarks Wendy had inflicted through the years. And best of all, Wendy's snide words in the ladies' room yesterday had given her the push to change her image. If the woman only knew. That was the greatest revenge.

"Yes. It's me," Tori crooned. "But to go along with my new status as extremely *successful,*" she stressed the word, "and quite *wealthy,* I've decided to use the name Tori."

Wendy shrugged, and Tori bit her lip to keep from smiling. If Wendy had wanted to give the appearance of nonchalance, she failed badly. Her beet-red face gave her away.

"Where's Irene?" Wendy asked. "I need her to do some typing for me."

"Family emergency. I'm not sure when she'll be back." Tori sat down behind the receptionist's desk again. "I'm afraid you're going to have to do your own typing today."

Uttering a noise that sounded like "Humph," Wendy turned on her heel and marched to her desk. Tori caught Dain's eye, and they laughed together.

"Lunch today?" he asked. "Dinner tonight?"

"Whoa!" Tori held up her hand. "Aren't you moving a bit fast, Mr. Becker?" A little voice cautioned her that they'd worked out of the same office for four years. Until yesterday, he hadn't said more than two words to her that weren't business related. Then another little voice countered that she'd been attracted to him for a long time—even before she'd started dating Eddie—so why shouldn't she accept what was being offered to her now?

A born optimist, the years had taught her to be doubting and distrustful. That negative attitude needed to be banished along with the dowdy clothes, the mousy hair, and the old-fashioned name.

She said, "Let's start with lunch and take it from there."

"I'll take it any way I can get," Dain said, running his finger down her arm, making her shiver. "See you later, beautiful."

Tori twirled the strands of cheese-coated fettucini around her fork and brought it to her lips. Savoring the creamy Alfredo sauce, spicy with oregano and pepper, she said, "This is delicious."

Dain took a sip of wine. "Guillermo's is the best Italian restaurant in West Palm. I'm surprised you haven't been here before."

"Well, I. . . ." She wasn't going to tell him that her restaurant dining experiences were limited to fast-food chains—that to her ex-boyfriend, eating Italian meant calling out for pizza.

Dain cupped his chin in his hands and snared her gaze with his improbably green, leaf-green eyes. "I just can't get over the change in you."

Smiling, Tori laid down her fork and pulled on a springy blond curl. "I've always wanted to be a blonde, but I never had the nerve to give it a try."

Dain studied her with mesmerizing intensity. His smile sparkled like a toothpaste commercial. His voice crooned a sexy baritone. Nevertheless, she felt her attention being tugged toward the door almost as if someone were pulling an invisible rope, and she had been lassoed to the other end.

Tori saw Matt Claussen standing beside the hostess's stand, his eyes riveted on her. Even across the room, she could see how well his gray summer-weight suit fit his tall, broad-shouldered body. Flustered, unaccountably embarrassed, and inordinately pleased, she barely heard Dain's next words as Matt strode toward their table with his confident gait.

Dain said, "You should have bleached your hair sooner. It's made a world of diff—" He swiveled around when Matt clamped his hand on his shoulder.

"Claussen! Hello. Here for lunch?"

Matt nodded, never releasing Tori from the

force of his gaze. "Meeting a client. I got here a little early. Hello, Victoria." He stood just behind Dain so that the realtor had to keep his body awkwardly twisted to see him.

"Hello, Matt." Tori gulped her wine, needing to moisten her suddenly dry throat. Still, she couldn't break the rope that tied her gaze to Matt's.

"For a minute I wasn't sure it was you. You look so different. But even across the room—"

"We're trying to eat our lunch, Claussen," Dain cut in. "If you'll excuse us . . ."

"Actually, my client won't be here for another half hour, so I'll join you for a glass of wine. Toast to Victoria's new look." He hooked the leg of a chair with his foot and pulled it out.

"We were having a nice quiet meal until . . ."

But Dain's protestations were in vain. Matt had already slid into the chair to Tori's right and motioned the waiter to bring him a glass.

Dain opened his mouth, then closed it again, obviously realizing any further objections would be a waste of breath. Matt had already topped his glass with zinfandel from the carafe on the table.

Finally Dain said, "Tori and I would like to be alone, Claussen. You're intruding on our date." He turned his back to Matt and leaned toward Tori, flashing his toothy grin at her.

"Date, is it?" Matt arched one dark eyebrow, and the only word Tori could think of to describe his expression was sardonic. He raised his glass. "To you, Victoria. Continued success."

Ignoring Matt's toast, Dain covered Tori's hand with his as if staking his claim. "Yes, Claussen. This is a date. The first of many I expect."

Matt's eyes bored into Tori's soul. He made her feel as if somehow she were betraying him. Ridiculous. But she eased her hand from beneath Dain's and curved it around the stem of her wine goblet. She wiped her other hand on the red silk fabric covering her thigh. Two men had never squabbled over her before. It was very flattering. In a way, she enjoyed it. But mostly she felt uncomfortable—flushed and fidgety and wishing they would stop.

Static crackled from Matt and encircled her. Her insides fluttered. She couldn't raise her glass, her fingers trembled so badly. If Dain had danced a jig on the table, she wouldn't have noticed.

"Tori. Tori!" Dain called, trying to get her attention. Reluctantly, her eyes focused on him. He gave her his sexy smile.

He certainly knew how to push her buttons. But at that moment, her body was tingling so much, she couldn't tell which stimulus was causing what reaction. Even the wine she'd gulped hadn't dulled her senses.

Dain said, "Your pasta's getting cold."

Tori understood that Dain's husky whisper was really saying their relationship was getting cold, and he wanted to warm it up again.

She forced her attention back to the food. Before, it had tasted like well-seasoned fettucini; now, it tasted like cardboard. Cold, congealed cardboard. She glanced at Matt sipping his wine. His blue eyes were sparkling, and he had the smug look of a cat that has swallowed a goldfish. The blood rushing through her veins seemed to simmer, then heat to a boil.

Why was he trying to ruin everything? First he wanted to curtail her spending. Now he was butting into her social life. She stabbed the fettucini so hard, her fork clattered against the plate.

Matt reached over and gently touched a blond curl. "Very pretty. Soft."

The fire already raging in her blood heated up several more degrees. He rubbed the tresses between thumb and forefinger, and she saw a glimmer of raw emotion in his eyes. When his thumb brushed her cheek, she jumped as if scalded and instinctively her head tilted toward him.

From somewhere a long way off, she heard Dain's bark of rage and came to her senses. She snapped her head back, pulling her hair out of Matt's grasp. He had some nerve, touching her hair so intimately!

Using sarcasm as a defense against her befuddlement, she cleared her throat and said, "I'm so glad you approve."

"Why'd you do it?"

Dain broke in. "Because she wanted to be even more beautiful than she already was. As if that was possible."

Sweet words, Tori knew, but hogwash. Yet she loved the sound of them.

"Makes you look different," Matt said. "Don't you agree, Becker?"

Dain nodded. "That's what I've been trying to tell her. The change is remarkable. Like night and day."

Suppressing a chuckle, she looked at Dain. The more he spoke, the more he put his foot in his mouth, and he didn't even know it.

"I was tired of my conservative persona." She turned to Matt. "It was time for a change, especially now that I can afford it."

"You could've colored your hair before you earned all that money," Matt said, "if you'd really wanted to."

"I guess I never really had the nerve to try it before. Something about the security of having a healthy bank account makes it easier for me to take chances."

Matt shook his head. "You'd better be careful *who* you take your chances with. Once you've spent all your money, we'll see if your new beau really thinks you're beautiful." He looked meaningfully at Dain. Then he scraped back his chair and walked away.

"Now see here, Claussen . . ." Dain was halfway out of his chair, obviously intending to go after

Matt who had already made his way to the hostess's stand.

Tori put a restraining hand on Dain's arm. "Don't make a scene. Please. Let him go." Her hand trembled so badly, she drew it away and clenched it into a fist. The nerve of that man, she thought, watching Matt follow a host to a table. How dare he speak to her that way!

"He insulted me," Dain spluttered.

"He insulted me, too. And I'm asking you to forget it. Please. For me." Chivalry wasn't dead, she thought with relief when Dain sat down again. Her anger began to fizzle away like a deflating balloon. After all, didn't she have what she'd been wanting? Wasn't she with Dain?

She planned to enjoy the rest of this meal with the man she'd been attracted to for a long time. Yet if it were physically possible, she'd wrap her fingers around Matt's strong neck and squeeze until . . .

Closing her eyes, she visualized her fingers on his throat, but they weren't squeezing. They were caressing the warm skin, her fingertips running gently over his Adam's apple, her fingers tangling in his thick dark hair. . . . Swallowing hard, she opened her eyes, and the image disappeared.

Instead, she saw Dain glare across the room toward the table where Matt had been seated. "A hundred years ago," Dain said, "I would have slapped his cheek with my glove."

"Times have changed, Dain. Bet you don't even

have a glove." Her attempt to levity was wasted on him.

He shook his head. "That man's behavior was insufferable. No Southern gentleman would put up with it."

Tori laughed at his indignation. "This is modern day Florida, not eighteenth century Louisiana."

She stifled her amusement when she saw the dangerous flare in his eyes. The last thing she wanted was to fan the flames of his outrage. She was angry enough for both of them. Her eyes narrowed. She'd deal with Matt Claussen herself. And, she vowed, it wouldn't be a pretty scene.

Across the room, Matt intercepted yet another glare from Dain. He shrugged it off. The moment he'd approached their table, he knew Dain Becker would be furious. It was Victoria's anger he regretted. The way things were going between them, he should have anticipated her reaction.

When he'd walked into the restaurant, his eyes had been drawn to Victoria like a bee to an orange blossom, although for a split second he hadn't recognized her. Then, when he realized she was with Becker, he felt his entire body cringe with distaste. Lovely Victoria with that jerk. He knew he had to do something, and so he had.

Matt held up the menu in front of him and peeked over the top. Victoria and that snake were eating dessert. They'd be leaving soon. At least they were having lunch, not dinner. They'd have to go back to the office. He wouldn't be taking her home, wouldn't be taking her to bed. He scowled and his eyebrows came together in a long thick line. No, Becker wouldn't be taking her to bed. Not now, anyway. Not ever, if he had anything to say about it. Unbidden, his mind saw Becker's hands on Tori's soft body, his fingers caressing her—Matt ran a finger around his collar. He couldn't breathe.

He watched as Dain stood up and went around to help Victoria out of her chair. The weasel stroked her hair. Matt's fingers clenched the menu so tight they creased the heavy paper. Victoria glanced over her shoulder and Matt quickly raised the menu. He didn't want her to see him watching her. But he knew he had to think of something to undo the damage he'd done a little while ago. Instead of driving a wedge between Dain and Victoria as he'd wanted, he'd managed to widen the gap between Victoria and himself.

When Tori returned to the office, Irene leaned across her desk and whispered in a conspiratorial tone, "Did you have a nice lunch? Was Dain all you expected?"

Tori pulled a chair close to Irene's, sat in it, and said, "Lunch was delicious. Dain was wonderful, but . . ."

"But what?" Irene's eyes gleamed.

The receptionist had been a good friend, and Tori knew she could be trusted with her secrets—

such as they were. "But Matt Claussen showed up."

Irene chuckled. "And that's bad?"

Tori pursed her lips like a preacher contemplating sin. "He sat at our table like he owned the place. Helped himself to a glass of wine and insulted us."

"Insulted you. How?"

As Tori described the scene in the restaurant objectively, careful to leave out the conflict of emotions that had tilted her perspective, she saw the humor in the situation. Irene's chuckles became out-and-out laughter, and Tori joined in.

She flashed a glance at Dain's desk, glad he was out with a client. If he saw them laughing, he'd know why. He wouldn't consider the situation funny.

"So the carpetbagger angered the impoverished Southern gentleman." Irene wiped her eyes. "Dain always did have a quick temper. Remember the time—" The phone rang, interrupting her reminiscence, and Tori strolled back to her desk.

She pulled her appointment book toward her but didn't open it. Instead she steepled her fingers and rested her chin on the point, gazing at Dain's empty chair. The luncheon had been going so well until Matt barged in. After all these years, Dain was finally interested in her. If she'd known a change of hair color was all it took to make him discover her, she'd have done it sooner. Maybe she hadn't been ready for him earlier. Maybe she needed the bolstered ego her money bought.

Now with the self-confidence born of her newly acquired wealth and attractiveness, she could accept his advances as her due. After all, wasn't she as pretty as Wendy? More successful than any of them? A little voice, niggling at her subconscious, warned her to suspect Dain's sudden interest. Brushing that thought from her mind like a pesky fly, she shook her head and opened the appointment calendar.

She was scheduled to see the property of an elderly woman in Boca Raton who had been trying to sell her house for two years. Yes indeed, she thought. She would specialize in expensive, hard-to-sell properties. The commissions wouldn't be frequent, but when they came, they'd be huge. Then, when the market turned around, she'd have the contacts and a solid reputation.

She checked her watch. One o'clock. Her appointment wasn't until three-thirty. More than enough time to drive down to Boca and kill a couple of hours in Bloomingdale's.

She picked up her battered old purse. You're the next to go, she mentally told the handbag. The intercom buzzed.

"Matt Claussen on line four," Irene told her.

"I'm not here."

"I already told him you were. Speak to him, Vic—ah—Tori. Hear him out."

Tori screwed up her face childishly but hit the button for line four. "Hello, Matt. I'm sorry I don't have time to talk to you now. I have an appointment in Boca."

"Stay out of the mall." The words sprang unbidden from Matt's lips, and he cursed himself for speaking before thinking. He wasn't calling to provoke her.

"Where I spend my time and money is none of your business," she said. "I have better things to do than to listen to—"

"I'm sorry," he cut in. Maybe he could make amends.

"What?" Tori sounded surprised, as if the last thing she expected from him was an apology.

"I'm sorry about this afternoon. I didn't mean to ruin your . . . date. But when I spotted you, looking like an angel, your beautiful golden hair like a halo, I had to speak to you." Matt held the phone close to his mouth and lowered his voice, modulating like a disk jockey. "But then I didn't know what to say."

If only he meant those wonderful, flattering words, Tori thought. Despite his protestations to the contrary, he certainly knew which words could turn a woman's head.

"You?" she asked. "I'll bet you've never in your life been at a loss for words." She tried to sound stern, but she was succumbing to his sweet talk.

"Let me make it up to you. Dinner tonight?"

"No." Then, trying to soften the harshness of her refusal, she added, "I don't know what time I'll be back."

When Matt had decided to make the call, he knew winning her over wasn't going to be easy. So he wasn't going to give up now. "I could meet you in Boca."

"Don't be silly."

He tightened his lips before saying, "Tomorrow night then."

"Why are you so persistent?"

"Because . . . I want to see you."

That was the point of the call. He wanted to be with her. Ever since he'd met her, he'd been interested in her, curious to discover what kind of woman was hiding behind the facade of black suits and low-heeled shoes. What she was really thinking behind those doe-sweet eyes and the placid expression on her heart-shaped face. He'd asked her out several times, but she hadn't taken him seriously. Reluctant to push her, biding his time, he'd waited for the right moment. The right moment had finally arrived. He hoped it hadn't passed. Becker was proving to be a formidable rival.

He sensed she felt the strong current that surged between them whenever they were together, just as he had. He wanted to see where those feelings would take them. And he wanted to make sure she didn't throw away all her money. Certainly not on that fiscally irresponsible, womanizing ass, Dain Becker.

Tori picked up a pencil and threaded it round and round between her fingers like a miniature baton. "You've seen me at least once a week for the past year. What's changed?" She knew exactly what had changed. Now she had money, lots of money. And he wanted a percentage of it.

"You've changed, Victoria. That's for sure."

"I hope so, Matt. By the way, I've decided not to use your investment services."

"That's your right. But please find someone else. I could recommend—"

"I'll find my own advisor, thank you."

"If that's what you want. But until you do, don't overspend, and for heaven's sake, watch out for gigolos."

"Gigolos!" Tori jabbed the pencil at the appointment book. A long black line slashed across the page. She choked back a laugh. "You can't be serious. They went out with high-button shoes."

"High-button shoes are coming back into fashion. Just be careful, Victoria."

"I can take care of myself."

"Victoria." Her name on his lips was a seductively whispered plea.

All the resistance oozed out of her. "Okay," she conceded. "I'll watch out for wolves in sheep's clothing, and I'll hire a financial advisor."

"And you'll stay out of the malls until you do?"

She crossed her fingers. "And I'll stay out of the malls." *Until I get to Boca,* she amended silently.

"And you'll have dinner with me tomorrow?"

In order to hold on to her anger, she deliberately reminded herself of the hurtful things he'd said to her in the restaurant. "Absolutely not. Not tonight. Not tomorrow. Not ever."

She hung up before he could pressure her further. She'd been close to weakening. She didn't want to go out with him, didn't want to find out if his touch really did kindle those fires inside her.

When they weren't discussing her finances, they got along very well. Too well. Although she was interested in Dain, the crosscurrent that surged between her and Matt was undeniable. Sooner or later, she'd have to confront those feelings, but not yet. Not until she felt more in control of her destiny—not until she had a chance to see where her relationship with Dain was headed. Not until she spent more of her money.

Chapter Four

Tori grabbed her multiple listing book and her purse and hurried to the exit as if pursued by demons. "I'm going to Boca," she called to Irene as she passed the receptionist's desk. "I'll be gone for the rest of the day." If Matt tried to call her again, she'd be out of reach—unless he called her on the car phone!

Driving south to Boca Raton, she grudgingly admitted that an indescribable something smoldered between her and Matt. But he was always so serious and wanted to curtail her fun. Dain, on the other hand, was amusing and devil-may-care, just the sort of companion her fun-starved soul was seeking.

Matt had made his disapproval of Dain quite clear. Was he jealous? Her ego was stroked by her unaccustomed role of *femme fatale*. She hadn't realized how much the change of hairstyle and wardrobe would transform her life.

Did she have to choose between the men or could she have both? Did she want both? Either?

Neither? The next few weeks would be interesting. A grin tugged at the corners of her mouth as she exited the highway.

When she parked the car in the lot of the Town Center Mall in Boca, she felt a tiny pang of guilt. After all, she had—sort of—promised Matt no shopping.

She browsed through the satellite shops. Knowing she could buy anything she wanted made looking as much fun as buying. As if Matt were standing beside her, whispering in her ear, she heard his warning. "Keep out of the malls. Don't spend so much." She'd wait until she had a good financial advisor before spending any more big bucks. Maybe she'd ask Matt to recommend someone, or maybe she'd use his services after all. Her heart fluttered. If she did business with him, she'd have a good excuse to see him.

Holding a silk blouse against her chest, she could almost feel Matt's hot breath fanning the wisps of hair on her neck. Damn. The man had insinuated himself into her conscience. She couldn't wait to see him again, just to get him out of her system.

In the end, when she left the mall with the same old purse tucked under her arm, her hands were empty of shopping bags. The only purchases she'd made all afternoon were a romance novel and a pack of chewing gum.

* * *

Later that afternoon Tori acquired an exclusive listing for a lovely house on the Intracoastal Waterway. As Mrs. Bergman, its elderly owner, showed her through the spacious bedrooms and airy living areas, Tori felt her excitement grow. Although this house was much smaller than the property she'd sold to the talk show hostess, it was large by most people's standards. The commission from its sale wouldn't be as much, but it would be substantial.

"We remodeled just five years ago," Mrs. Bergman said as they walked into a modernized kitchen. Almond colored appliances twinkled in the sunlight streaming through the window which overlooked a small, pretty garden. "There are five bedrooms and three full baths. My late husband and I raised two children here. I love this place. I have mixed feelings about giving it up, but it's too big for me to manage now."

"The right person will love it like you do."

"Do you really think you can sell it?" Mrs. Bergman's brow wrinkled like old parchment. "It's been on the market for two years now."

Tori's heart went out to the gray-haired woman. Of course, first and foremost this was a business arrangement, and Tori always conducted herself in a professional manner. But she really wanted to make the sale for Mrs. Bergman's sake.

An hour later the signed contract for her exclusive listing of the house was tucked away in Tori's briefcase, and she was driving home. Into a tape recorder, she listed the property's major selling points and some marketing ideas.

". . . It backs on the Intracoastal Waterway and has a private boat dock. Its relative seclusion might interest a celebrity, either an entertainer or sports figure. Ads should be placed in trade newspapers and magazines."

Yawning, she switched off the recorder and tossed it onto the passenger's seat. Holding the steering wheel with one hand, she massaged her tight neck and shoulder muscles. It had been a long, exciting day topped off by the long drive home. Exhaustion washed over her like the warm bath she craved. She gripped the wheel and concentrated on the road.

At last she steered her car through the gates of her condominium complex. Relieved to be home, she was envisioning herself in that relaxing bath when her headlights lit up a sleek white Cadillac parked in the spot in front of her unit. She muttered an unladylike oath. She hated when someone parked in her space.

Then her heart flip-flopped. The car was Matt Claussen's. What was he doing here?

She slid her BMW into the adjacent space and saw him sitting on her front steps as if he belonged there, spotlighted like a movie star in the glare of her porch lamp. His usually styled hair had curled up from the humidity. One particularly errant wave had fallen across his forehead, adding to his sexy, movie star appearance.

Her instinctive reaction to seeing him was pure delight. A smile floated to her lips. Her breath caught. When he jumped to his feet and sprinted toward her, she wanted to reach out to him. Then she remembered he was opposed to everything that would make her happy.

The smile faded. She felt a pang of disappointment that things couldn't be different between them. But she had to accept the reality of the situation. Besides, wasn't she angry with him? Hadn't he tried to ruin her date with Dain? Hadn't his glib admonitions ruined her shopping spree in Boca?

Mentally reciting all the reasons to be annoyed with him, Tori took a deep breath. Slowly, she reached back to unlock the car door, then edged it open. By the time she got out, he was standing beside the car.

"What are you doing here?" she demanded.

"You were upset when you took off for Boca this afternoon. I wanted to make sure you got home okay." He peered into the car then pushed the door shut.

"I wasn't upset. I was angry." Hands on hips, her mouth twisted in forced anger, she said, "You're checking up on me." When he ignored her comment and looked into the backseat, she asked, "What are you looking for, hitchhikers?"

"Packages. Thought I'd help you carry them in. Are they in the trunk? Give me the keys, and I'll get them for you."

71

Her annoyance at his presumption twisted her stomach. How arrogant of him to assume she'd bought out the store. Hadn't he told her not to shop? Did he think she was so contrary that the word "don't" was reason enough to make her "do"?

"There aren't packages." Now she sorely regretted not buying that silk blouse. It would have served Matt right. She brushed past him and hurried up the shrub-lined path. "Sorry to disappoint you."

"I'm not disappointed." He followed right behind her. "I'm pleased. It means you're finally listening to me, or even better, you're listening to the more sensible side of yourself."

She stopped at her front door and looked over her shoulder. A compliment? From Matt? Even a backhanded compliment sounded good coming from him. She didn't know how to respond. "Thanks for coming over." Her voice gentled a bit but still held a biting edge. "As you can see, I'm fine. Just tired. Good night." She reached into her purse for her keys, but before she could pull them out he took her arm in his loose grasp.

"Wait a minute, Victoria."

"Tori," she corrected.

"Actually I came to apologize for my . . . er—"

"Boorish behavior," she supplied.

"Not boorish exactly, but yeah, my less than gentlemanly actions when you were with that jerk Becker."

"You're sticking your foot right back into your mouth, Mr. Claussen. Are you here to apologize or to make things worse?"

He propped his hand on the wall just beside her head. "Invite me in, and I'll tell you."

She gave a little gasp. He was close. Too close. She could smell his cologne. See the light spattering of crisp hairs on his bare arm and the fine lines that crinkled around his blue eyes when he smiled. Feel his masculine heat. She stepped back and found herself wedged against the door. Her fingers trembled when she reached behind her and grasped the doorknob.

His scent wrapped itself around her in a velvet mist. She couldn't breathe, could hardly think. She swallowed hard and forced herself to look down, away from the invitation in his eyes. Her gaze fell on his initialed belt buckle, then strayed slightly lower. Heat rushed to her cheeks and coiled through her body.

She lurched away and fumbled for her keys, but her fingers didn't have enough strength to unlock the door. Calmly, he took the key from her, inserted it in the lock, then pulled the door open. He stepped to one side so that she could go in first.

As he started to cross the threshold, she turned and faced him. "I don't think . . . this isn't a good time. I've had a long day, and as I said, I'm tired. I—"

"I'll bet you haven't eaten. We could go out

somewhere. Or if you're too tired, we'll order pizza and have it delivered."

When she hesitated, he continued, "What'll it be? I've been waiting for you a long time. Maybe you're not hungry, but I sure am. A thick juicy steak with a bottle of chardonnay. Mmmmm." He wiggled his eyebrows and licked his lips.

Her mouth watered. A long time had passed since that . . . interesting . . . lunch, and she was hungry. With a sigh of defeat, she took a step back. "Pizza," she said. "I can't bear the thought of going out again. Come on in," she added grudgingly, opening the door wider.

As Matt strolled into her home, he looked around. The walls were white; the tiled floor was white. But splashes of color proved what he'd suspected all along. The woman had a sensual nature she'd been hiding beneath all that conservative rigamarole.

He walked across a shaggy red and white area rug and sat on a white crushed velvet sofa. Flowery needlepoint pillows in vivid reds and greens and blues were wedged into the corners and along the back.

He lifted one of the pillows. "Did you do this?" When she nodded, he said, "My mother needlepoints. She always has a canvass in her lap. You too?"

"No." She frowned. "Unfortunately, I don't have time any more. Too busy earning a living."

She turned away. "I'm calling for the pizza. What do you want on it?"

"Everything but mushrooms and anchovies." He crossed his right ankle over his left thigh and leaned back, trying to appear nonchalant while contemplating his next words.

Obviously she was as prickly as a cactus where he was concerned; and, he conceded, she had every right to be. He sure had made a mess of things that afternoon in the restaurant and hadn't done much to improve matters over the phone or just now, either. His major personality flaw, as he saw it, was his inability to be tactful when he needed to be honest—especially with Victoria.

The melodious flow of her voice as she ordered the pizza washed over him like an aria, and he closed his eyes, listening, enjoying. While he'd waited for her to come home, he'd planned what he was going to say. But, of course, the moment he opened his mouth, all the wrong words tumbled out. Not this time. The next sentence he uttered would be thought out and designed to charm.

He heard the click of her heels as she came back into the living room, and he opened his eyes.

She said, "I'm going to change into something more comfortable."

He lifted an eyebrow, opened his mouth to speak, then closed it against the words that struggled to get out. But the damage had been done. Color flooded her cheeks as she whirled around and went into what he assumed was her bedroom. When he heard the turn of her lock, he chuckled quietly. He'd have to teach her that just because he wasn't the most tactful man on the block, it didn't mean he couldn't be trusted.

While he waited — and wondered if she would come out of her haven — he continued his inspection of her home. A short and narrow breakfast bar separated the kitchen area from the small dining nook to the side of the living room. White vertical blinds extended from a ceiling valance to the floor. He assumed it covered a sliding glass door to a terrace.

He started to get up to see what lay beyond the terrace when her door opened, and she stepped out. Just the sight of her reminded his body how much he wanted her. She wore a sundress that came to mid-thigh and was held up by skinny little straps. Unfortunately, the fabric hung straight down from her breasts and only hinted at the curves of her waist and hips. She'd pulled her honey colored hair back from her face and caught it up with a red ribbon that matched the flowers on her dress. Many's the time he'd imagined what she'd look like if she'd cast off those drab and dreary suits and wore something colorful and becoming. The reality was even more desirable than the fantasy.

"Want something to drink?" Her bare feet slapped against the tiles as she made her way to the kitchen. "I'm afraid all I have to offer is soda or lemonade. There might be a beer in the fridge, but I doubt it."

"Soda is fine. Whatever you've got. Water's good too." Matt sat on one of the stools in front of the breakfast bar. "Did they say how long the pizza would take?"

"About forty-five minutes." She glanced at the clock on the microwave.

"I hope you ordered a large. I could eat one all by myself."

"How about a salad?" She opened the refrigerator.

"I don't want you to go to any trouble."

"It's already made." She took out a large plastic container and started emptying greens into two wooden bowls.

After giving him a fork and pouring soda from a liter bottle into two glasses, she came around and perched on the other stool. "So how was your day?"

"Pretty good. Except, of course, when I was making an ass of myself in the restaurant." Liar, he called himself. That was the best part of his whole day—except that what he'd done had made her angry.

"Is that an apology?"

"Yup." He put down his fork and held out his hand. "Is it accepted?"

She made a wry face but let him wrap his fingers around hers. "I suppose," she said. "I—"

The phone rang and she pulled her hand out of Matt's grasp to pick it up. "Hello."

He made no attempt to give her privacy. When she said, "Oh, hi, Dain," he propped his elbow on the table and rested his chin on the back of his hand, watching her, overtly listening.

She turned her back to him, and although she kept her voice low, he heard every word she spoke to Becker. Didn't the woman know the guy was after her money? On the contrary, she seemed flattered by his attentions. How could he make her see what a jerk Becker was without making himself look bad?

Dain's voice, crooning into Tori's ear, said, "Let's do breakfast tomorrow. I want to start my day off right."

Feeling Matt's eyes on her, she could barely comprehend what Dain was saying. "Um, breakfast?" She spoke softly into the mouthpiece. "Yeah. Sure. Why not."

"Till tomorrow then," Dain said.

"Yes. I'll see you in the morning. Thanks for calling." She hung up and turned to Matt. "At least you could have gone into the living room."

He pointed to his salad. "I didn't know if you allowed eating on the couch."

She waggled her finger at him as if he were a stubborn child. "You wanted to be sure you heard everything I said."

"I don't give a damn what you say to Becker as long as you know what a jerk he is."

"He is not." Her eyes flashed. "He's sensitive and caring."

"Oh yeah, he cares." He didn't dare tell her that she was beautiful when she was angry—but she was so lovely she took his breath away. "He cares about your money."

"That's not true, Matt. You're the one who's interested in my money."

"You have a point there," he acknowledged. As she started to speak, he put out his hand and jumped in with, "But only professionally. It's my job to care about your money and make sure you get the best return from it. He's only concerned with how much you'll spend on him."

"That's simply not so."

He shook his head and raised his hand, the palm thrust out like a traffic cop's. "I didn't come here to argue. My goal was to make up. You just forgave me. Don't get angry again. Where were we when we were so rudely interrupted?"

Grasping her fingers, he traced his thumb in light circles over the sensitive spot between her thumb and forefinger. Her skin felt silky and as warm as sunshine.

For a moment, Tori allowed her hand to rest in his, enjoying the sensual contact. But when that all too familiar warmth cascaded through her, she pulled away. Matt shouldn't be affecting her that way.

"The pizza will be here any second." She gulped her soda and hiccupped. "Excuse me!"

"Shouldn't drink soda too fast." He grinned, pleased that he'd managed to defuse her anger. "How'd it go today?"

"Today?" Why couldn't she focus on anything but his denim-covered leg only a fraction of an inch from her own bare thigh? She shifted, and instead of the space between them increasing, skin brushed denim and ignited like a match on flint.

"Yeah," he said. His Adam's apple bobbed when he swallowed. "How did it go in Boca? At that house you were hoping to list. Did you get it?"

When she answered, her voice cracked. "Sure did." She cleared her throat, at the same time trying to free her body of those unwanted responses. "Sure did," she repeated. "It's a wonderful house."

"Is it a new listing?"

"Well, no." There he went again, pulling her down to earth by injecting the truth. "But I'm developing a marketing plan that I know will make a difference. Like that place in Palm Beach. After all, I only need one buyer."

Matt put his hand on her shoulder. Her animation was electric. It crackled through her pores and sizzled against his palm. How could anyone resist her?

"You can't miss, Victoria." The urge to tell her what she was doing to him was very strong. But before he could speak, the doorbell rang

"The pizza." Tori swiveled her stool and started to stand up.

He pushed her down gently. "I'll get it." As he opened the door, he pulled some bills from his pocket and paid the delivery boy.

While they ate, she continued to describe the house and her plans for marketing it. To her delight, he was extremely encouraging and supportive, even offering a few excellent suggestions.

When they were finished eating, he stood up, loaded their dishes into the dishwasher and wiped the counter. She watched him with widened eyes. He seemed as comfortable in the kitchen as he was in a business meeting, and she liked what she saw. Matt Claussen was multifaceted. Very different from other men she'd known. Perhaps she'd been too hasty when she'd formed her original opinion of him.

"Coffee?" she offered.

"No thanks. Feel like going out for dessert?"

She shook her head. "Not tonight. I haven't the strength to even slip on a pair of shoes. I just want to put my feet up and unwind." She strolled over to the sofa, plopped down on one of the plump pillows, and dropped her bare feet on the coffee table. As an invitation for Matt to join her, she tapped the cushion beside her.

He didn't hesitate. Within moments he was sitting next to her, his shoes off, and his feet, in sparkling white socks, were beside hers on the coffee table.

He laced his fingers behind his head and leaned back. Tori felt heat radiating from him—a heat that hinted at pleasures beyond her imagination, and it drew her like a Pandora's box. Her body seemed to tilt toward him although she knew she hadn't stirred.

"So," Matt said, "have you thought about what you're going to do about your money?"

Although Victoria didn't shift her position, Matt felt her immediate withdrawal from him. He closed his eyes. He'd done it again. If the air conditioner suddenly dropped down to zero, the room wouldn't have become any colder. He'd thought they'd reached the point in their association where he could safely bring up the topic of her investments. Was he ever wrong.

"Actually, yes," she said. "I've given it a lot of thought."

He held his breath while he waited for her to continue. If she turned him down now, he'd have to respect her decision. He'd lose his only excuse to continue seeing her, to teach her to trust him, to find out if that chemical tug he felt flowing between them would grow into something deep and real. She'd never accepted when he'd asked her out, and he had no reason to believe she'd date him now. While he waited for her answer, the suspense was choking him.

"I'm going to let you handle it for me. You've been highly recommended, and I'd be foolish to go with someone else, when I know you're the best."

His breath rasped through his teeth. "That's

great, Victoria." He took her hand. "I know you'll be very pleased with the job I do for you."

"Tori," she corrected automatically.

Tori let her hand rest in his, let his exuberance erase her misgivings, let his warmth seep into her. Knowing they'd have lots of arguments about the way she spent her money, she hoped she was doing the right thing. But she knew he would give her excellent financial advice.

In that far corner of her mind, the thought niggled that they'd see each other again because of their business relationship. And again.

Something cottony seemed to wrap around her heart.

He caressed the inside of her wrist, and the softness in her chest spread outward. She gave a half-hearted tug. To her surprise, she was freed. Confused by her feelings, she slowly lowered her feet to the floor and stood up. Immediately, he jumped up.

Covering her mouth, she yawned. "Now that's decided, it's time for me to call it a night. I'm really exhausted." While he put on his sneakers, she added, "Thanks for the pizza."

"Any time," Matt said as he followed her to the door. "Victoria—"

"Tori."

"I'll be in touch. About your portfolio, I mean." He opened the door. "Maybe over dinner sometime?"

He'd taken her hand again. Did he know about

the magic in his thumb? Of course he knew. Wasn't he using it to its best advantage? This time when she tugged, his fingers tightened their hold, and he traced the blue line of the vein at her wrist with light strokes. Could he feel the way her pulse was racing?

"Dinner? Maybe . . . sure . . . sometime. C—call me." She gulped.

His eyes studied her lips and she almost felt the pressure of a kiss. Coils of heat radiated through her body. If just imagining his lips on hers did all these wonderful things to her insides, what would it be like to actually feel his kiss? When he lowered his head, she subconsciously licked her lips, and for the length of a heartbeat enjoyed the anticipation. But the flame of his lips, when they finally touched her, scorched the sensitive curve of her throat where her pulse throbbed.

His kiss was soft and gentle, hard and strong. She closed her eyes and bent her head toward him. Then his touch left her, and she felt empty.

"Good night," she whispered. But she spoke to the air. He was already gone.

Chapter Five

When Tori strolled through the real estate office door, Dain jumped up from his chair and surprised her with a quick kiss on her lips.

"Hi, beautiful."

For once, he was at the office before she was. "What are you doing here so early?" She expected her pulse to quicken, her breath to catch, but all that happened was her nostrils flared slightly at the heaviness of his aftershave.

"Did you forget our breakfast date?" Dain sounded like a kid disappointed by Santa Claus.

"Breakfast?" She vaguely remembered that when he'd called the previous night, he'd mentioned something about catching a bite together in the morning. But with Matt sitting so close, listening to every word, only half—maybe even less than half—of her attention had been on their conversation.

"Don't tell me you forgot." The corners of Dain's mouth twisted before he curved them into a toothy smile. "Have you eaten?"

"Just some coffee and juice." She began walking to her desk, with Dain keeping pace at her side.

"Good," he said. "Then we can still get something to eat. Ready?" He took her arm and tried to urge her toward the door, but she pulled back.

"Dain. I'm sorry. I can't." She tossed her briefcase on her desk.

"Sure you can." While he waited for her decision, a flash of anger darkened his eyes before he covered up with an air of disappointment. "You aren't seeing a client, are you?"

"No." Why on earth was she putting him off? Hadn't she lusted for him—yes, lusted was the word, she admitted—for the better part of three years? Now she was finally getting what she wanted, and as usual, she was putting responsibility before fun.

"I promise to have you back by ten," Dain cajoled.

The whole point of changing her image was to let go of her conservative, overly conscientious self. Didn't the security of a healthy bank account give her the freedom to do what she wanted?

"Okay. But no later than ten."

"Great!" He grabbed her arm and ushered her through the exit before she could change her mind.

When they got to Dain's Firebird, he unlocked

the door on the driver's side, slid in and reached across the seats to open her door. Instinctively, Tori knew Matt would help a lady into a car the gallant, old-fashioned way. Every time she contrasted the two men, Dain came out the loser. She'd just have to stop comparing.

As they tore out of the driveway, Tori thought she saw Matt's white Cadillac coming from the opposite direction. Knowing his conscientiousness and efficiency, she guessed he'd already drawn up whatever papers were needed for her investments, and he'd come by the office to have her sign them. Too bad Dain had been in such a hurry. Had they left a minute or two later, she wouldn't have missed Matt. Now he'd have to wait.

And so would she, for that matter. She wanted to see him. To see if he'd been able to tame his unruly hair. To see the dimple notch into his cheek when he smiled at her. Although she was sitting beside the man with whom she expected to live out her fun fantasies, her disobedient heart yearned toward the driver of the staid, conservative automobile. Too bad, heart. Practical-minded Matt Claussen wasn't the man for her. His idea of fun was spending an evening with a ledger. She wanted more out of life than that.

Matt pulled his car into the parking lot of the

real estate agency just in time to see Becker drive away, and he was sure the woman sitting beside The Jerk was Victoria. What was the matter with her? Didn't she have any sense at all?

He had his hand on the gearshift, ready to reverse and follow them. Then he had second thoughts. He'd come a long way with her last night. If he showed up wherever Becker was taking her, everything he'd accomplished would be lost. He had to trust her judgment, had to trust she had enough sense not to hop into bed with the wrong man.

His stomach lurched at the thought of the two of them even kissing. If she was going to kiss anyone, make love with anyone, it would be with him, Matt.

He knew there was a chemistry between them, knew that she'd shared those feelings he'd experienced last night. Hadn't her pulse throbbed hot beneath his lips? Hadn't her hand practically melted into his? He felt a tightening in his groin just remembering.

Give her time, Claussen, he told himself. Give her space. Let her play the game her way. She was a sensible woman floating in the bubble of her newfound wealth and temporarily beguiled by Becker's pretty-boy good looks and smooth talking.

Before long, she'd come to her senses and land on her feet. When she did, she'd recognize the attraction between them for what it was. He had every confidence in her. If not, there were other women.

But none like her. No one but Victoria had expressive, luminous brown eyes that could sizzle with passion or flash with anger. No one else had a body that curved so perfectly against his. And her hair . . . well, he'd have to convince her that she didn't need to be blond to please a man, that her natural color suited her perfectly.

A horn tooted behind him; he was blocking the driveway. Victoria wasn't there, so he had no reason to go into the office building. He made a U-turn, exited the parking lot, and deliberately veered away in the opposite direction to the one taken by Becker and Victoria.

Tori pulled the vanity mirror down and looked at the reflection of the road through the rear windshield. Empty. No sleek white Cadillac had pulled in behind them. Perhaps Matt hadn't seen them. Or knowing what her response would be, he had the sense not to follow them. She sighed. With relief, she convinced herself.

"Tired?" Dain asked.

"Actually, a little. I was so excited about the new listing that I didn't sleep much last night." She didn't tell him that when she had finally fallen asleep, her dreams had been filled with Matt. Dreams that had left her with a vague longing that had nothing to do with the man beside her.

"Oh, you got a new listing?" He took his eyes away from the road to look at her and narrowly missed plowing into the pickup in front of them.

"Yes." Clutching the door handle, Tori glued her eyes on the road. One of them had to watch where they were going. "I thought I told you. In Boca." She started to tell him about the house but he cut in.

"You shouldn't have bothered. I brought some clients down there a couple of weeks ago, and they weren't at all interested."

She bristled. "Too bad you didn't show them this one. They would have snatched it up."

"I doubt it," he said, sounding as though he thought that if he couldn't sell a house, nobody could. He cut off a minivan, then patted her arm and amended his tactless statement with, "But if anyone can do it, Tori, you can." For a moment Tori had seen through a chink in his smooth veneer, but then it closed as if it had never been there. Once more she saw Dain as a handsome and glib man.

"Thanks," she said. "It's a wonderful hou—"

Tori stopped in mid-word as she was thrown against the door when Dain twisted the steering wheel sharply. The Firebird careened into the parking lot of a pancake restaurant and squealed to a stop in a spot with inches to spare. Although Dain opened the door slowly, he dinged the car next to them but showed no concern.

His hand, when he helped her out, was hot

and sweaty. As they walked to the restaurant, she gently pulled her fingers away, wiping them on her skirt when she thought he wasn't looking, then rubbing her shoulder where it had been bruised against the door.

During breakfast, she kept looking over Dain's shoulder at the entrance. She had the oddest feeling that Matt would turn up as he had the other day at lunch. Once, her heart leaped into her throat when she thought she saw him come in, but that man was wearing a huge cowboy hat and dark sunglasses which obscured his face. Still, the newcomer was Matt's height and build, and when he followed the hostess to a corner table, he walked with Matt's confident stride. Although he passed several feet away, she could have sworn she caught a whiff of Matt's lemon-lime aftershave. As soon as he was seated, he opened a newspaper and disappeared behind it.

Although he made no move to approach their table, Tori kept glancing at him, trying to penetrate his paper shield. She tried to concentrate on her date, but the man behind the newspaper tugged her attention as if she were a puppet and he controlled the strings. Deep in her heart, she knew he could only be Matt.

By the time she and Dain started on their second cups of coffee, the man still hadn't approached their table. Tori convinced herself she'd been mistaken. Matt hadn't shown up. Her spirits drooped.

She wasn't disappointed, she informed herself. Relieved. She'd been worried that he'd ruin her breakfast date, just as he'd ruined their lunch. That worry had prevented her from keeping up her end of their conversation. Matt had spoiled her breakfast as surely as if he'd been there.

"Tori? Tori." Dain tapped her hand. "Penny for your thoughts."

"What? Oh. I was just thinking about how much work I have ahead of me."

"Need help?"

"Thanks, but no. It's stuff I really have to take care of myself. Like composing advertising copy and calling it in to the newspapers and magazines I've targeted."

"Speaking of which . . ."

"Humm?"

"A buddy of mine is starting up a real estate newsletter," Dain said. "A magazine actually. Something glitzy and eye-catching."

"Oh? That sounds interesting."

"Yeah. I thought so, too. Thought I'd go into it with him. But we need a few more investors to get started." He reached across the table and rubbed his index finger up and down her arm.

"Oh?" Although she allowed his caress, her body didn't react at all. "How much are we talking about?" Immediately Tori remembered how insistent Matt had been about investing her capital. Here was an opportunity to invest and help a friend at the same time.

92

Dain mentioned a figure that made her head swim. "Wow. That's a lot of money. I suppose you've talked to a lot of people."

"Oh, yes. My buddy, Ellis Clayborne, has been involved in this project for quite a while. We just need a few thousand more to get us over the hump."

"Tell me the details."

She listened, intrigued with the concept of a monthly full-color publication devoted entirely to the real estate industry, with distribution throughout selected areas of the country. This was exactly the sort of vehicle she needed to reach other agents and the clientele she was hoping to attract.

When Dain was finished, he took a sip of coffee but pinned her with eyes as green as the money he was trying to charm her out of. "So what do you think? How much do you want to put up?"

"As I said, it sounds very interesting. I'll discuss it with Matt Claussen and get back to you in a day or two."

Dain slammed his mug on the table so hard that coffee sloshed over the rim. Tori jumped.

"What does Claussen have to do with it?" Dain demanded.

"He's my financial advisor."

"You don't need him." He softened his tone. "I'll help you."

Tori shook her head. "Of course I need him.

93

Even you've used his services from time to time."

"As a stock broker, not as an advisor." Burying Tori's hand under his, Dain insisted, "You're a smart woman. Why should you pay some guy a hefty commission just to tell you what you already know?"

"My expertise is in buying and selling houses, but I know very little about handling money. Unfortunately, I haven't had much money to handle before." She wriggled her fingers out from under his. His hand still felt clammy, and its hot dampness made her feel slightly uncomfortable. "So if there's a prospectus or some kind of proposal for the magazine that I can show Matt, I'll discuss it with him and let you know."

"Okay, honey," Dain said, leaning back in his chair. "If you don't trust my judgment, I guess I can try to understand. Just don't wait too long. Opportunities like this don't come along every day."

To Tori's ears, Dain's project sounded absolutely wonderful, and his enthusiasm was contagious. She'd convince Matt that this was a solid investment, maybe even get him to involve some of his other clients.

"It's not that I don't trust you," she said. "It's just that since I hired him, I should use him. I promise I'll get back to you about it soon."

"Okay. I guess I understand," he added grudgingly. "By the way, there's a beach party Saturday night. I'd like you to go with me. It'll be loads of fun."

She smiled. He'd said the magic word—fun. "Oh, that sounds wonderful. I'd love to go."

"Then it's a date. I'll let you know what time to meet me."

Meet him? Wasn't he going to pick her up? Was that the way new-fashioned, fun-loving people conducted their dates? Fine with her. When in Rome . . .

"Okay." She glanced at her watch. "Oh my goodness. We've been here and hour and a half. The whole morning's wasted."

"Wasted?" Dain asked, taking her hand again.

When he began stroking it, she waited in vain for the response she'd felt from Matt's gentle caress. Nothing. She didn't understand it. Wasn't this Dain Becker? The man who turned her to mush when he smiled at her across the office. Changing her image couldn't have caused her insides to change too.

"I'm insulted." He pouted slightly. "An hour and a half in your company is more valuable to me than work. I thought you felt the same."

She smiled. "Oh, Dain. I didn't mean it that way. If course I value our time together, it's just that—"

"I know. It's just that you have publication deadlines you want to meet so you can sell another old house."

She stood up. "It's not just another old house,

it's a gem of a property whose owner is reluctantly selling it." To Tori, the Bergman property was much more than just any old house. The elderly owner's sadness, her love for the home she had to give up, struck a responsive chord in Tori. She intended to make the sale as stress free for the lady as possible. "It's my job to find someone to buy it who will appreciate it as much as she does."

"Sure. Sure." Dain got to his feet and tossed coins on the table for a tip. "And it's your job to make a commission on the sale."

His callousness rankled. He hadn't even bothered to ask her about the house. Even if his interest wasn't personal, he was a real estate agent who should want to show it to potential buyers. If he was the agent who sold the house, he'd be the one to split the commission with her. Her mind swirling with indignation, she waited without comment while he paid the bill.

As she followed him back to the car, she scanned the parking lot, looking for Matt's Cadillac. Her pulse rate increased when she thought she spotted it. Then she noticed another large white auto. Then another. Maybe one was his. Maybe not. She couldn't be certain—except her strongest instincts assured her that Matt Claussen was the man in the restaurant.

Tori was sorting through the photos of

the house in Boca Raton when Matt phoned.

"Hi." As if he were beside her, Tori became acutely aware of the spot on her neck which his lips had so gently brushed the night before. She reached up to touch it.

"I've been doing some research," Matt said, "and I'm ready to start planning your portfolio. There are some ideas I want to pass by you. Can you come to my office this afternoon? It would be much more convenient to talk here, since everything we need to look at will be at hand, but mostly because we'll have privacy here."

Tori had hoped his reasons for calling were personal, not business. Her disappointment surprised her. "Well, I . . ." she waffled.

Wendy sashayed by. At that moment, privacy sounded very good.

"Okay, Matt. What time?"

Later that day, at the agreed time, Tori crossed the drawbridge to Palm Beach. She found a parking space in front of the building that housed Matt's office and nodded her approval. Very well located, she thought. Just a few blocks from the Flagler Museum and easily accessible for his Palm Beach clients — people who would be very impressed by his fancy address. And West Palm Beach was just the other side of Lake Worth.

The building boasted the Spanish style of architecture prevalent on the island, and the motif had been carried through in the office decor.

Tile floors, leather chairs, wrought iron lighting fixtures, and a heavy darkwood desk for Matt's secretary. Before Tori could identify herself to the woman, Matt came out of his office and greeted her.

"Come in." He touched her arm with incendiary results. "Sit down. Something to drink? Coffee. Cola?"

"A cola sounds wonderfully refreshing." Even though it was late in the day, it was still hot, but not as hot as Tori's feverish skin. What would happen when he actually caressed her?

He crossed the room to a mini-refrigerator, took out a can, then plucked a Styrofoam cup from a stack on top of it. As he walked back to her, he poured the soda into the cup.

When she took the cold drink from him, she held it to her brow. As she felt her temperature return to normal, she thought she'd better be careful. Her life was in danger of splintering off onto paths she'd neither planned nor anticipated.

To distract herself, she glanced around. Here, too, the decor had a Spanish flair, but this, she realized, was more Southwestern than the Moorish influence in Palm Beach. A Navajo rug was spread across the tile floor. The oil painting of a cattle roundup on the wall behind Matt's big desk looked so real, she could almost smell the dry dust. In one corner, a tall spiny cactus stood sentinellike in a Mexican pot.

The only item hanging on the coatrack was

the jacket to his dark suit. She noticed sun-glasses peeping out of the breast pocket. All that was missing was a cowboy hat.

She glanced at him sharply. Riffling through some papers, he seemed unaware of her scrutiny. Were the glasses in his pocket the same ones the man in the pancake restaurant had worn? It was certainly possible. She'd be willing to bet the commission on her next sale that the cowboy hat was in the Cadillac.

"What's the matter?" Matt asked.

"The matter?"

"You were shaking your head."

"Oh." She smiled. "Just thinking."

"About what?"

"Were you in the restaurant this morning?" she blurted.

"What restaurant?" His eyes were riveted on what appeared to be an annual report.

"The one where Dain and I had breakfast."

"So that was you in Becker's car this morning."

"You saw me? Did you follow us?"

Because he tried so hard to look innocent, Tori was convinced of his guilt.

He poked his chest. "Me?" His eyes danced with mischief. "After what happened yesterday at lunch? You just forgave me. I don't want you to be angry with me again."

She shook her head doubtfully. Why borrow trouble? If Matt said he wasn't there, she had no reason to doubt him. Yet . . . he hadn't actually said he wasn't there.

"Do you own a cowboy hat?"

He didn't miss a beat. "Sure. Most former rodeo riders do. Why?"

"Were you really in a rodeo?"

"For a while. One or two, but when I realized I was spending more time under the horse than on it, I decided enough was enough."

Tori looked at him through new eyes. Maybe he wasn't so practical after all. Somewhere deep inside him was an adventurous streak. If only she could tap it . . .

Later, when they were discussing investments, she mentioned Dain's business proposal.

Matt exploded like a firecracker on the Fourth of July. "I told you before, The Jerk is just after your money. There's the proof."

She jumped up. "Obviously this isn't going to work."

He hurried around his desk and took her arm before she could escape through the door.

"Sit down. I'm sorry I called the . . . Becker a jerk."

She sat but kept her eyes narrowed and waited while he tried to untangle himself from this latest verbal pratfall.

"You do have to concede that Becker's scheme smells a little fishy," he said, sitting on the edge of his desk.

"It does not. It's an excellent plan. The real

estate industry needs the type of publication his friend is planning. Think how much easier and cheaper it will be to reach prospective clients."

"Cheaper for other realtors, perhaps. But it'll cost you, as an investor, all your money."

"I won't invest it all. Give me some credit for common sense. I would never put all my eggs in one basket. That's why I wanted to *discuss* this with you first." She emphasized the word discuss because the tone of their conversation had deteriorated very quickly.

"Okay. Let's *discuss* it."

Trying to sound logical and sensible, she outlined the plan for Matt, much as Dain had done with her. "He'll be bringing me a prospectus which I'll pass on to you," she concluded.

Matt steepled his fingers and tapped his index finger against his mouth. She watched, fascinated, and remembered the warmth of that mouth on her skin and speculated about how it would feel against hers.

She cleared her throat. "Well? What do you think?"

"I can't really advise you until I see the prospectus. But from what I know about Becker, my gut tells me to steer clear."

"Well, my gut tells me to go ahead with it."

"I guess we're at a stalemate. It's your money, of course. I can only advise. All the final decisions are yours."

"Okay."

"Do you want me to finish explaining what I've come up with?"

"Of course."

He handed her a file folder then pulled a chair close to hers. Totally professional now, he spread some papers on the desk in front of them.

After about twenty minutes of mathematic computations and complicated explanations, he said, "That's about it." He stacked the papers back into the portfolio. "Take this home and look it over. Give it a few days to sink in, then we'll discuss it again. By then I should have had a chance to look over Becker's stuff, and we can factor that into your portfolio. If you do decide to go with him, I suggest keeping your investment small. Five thousand dollars should be the maximum."

Tori was reluctant to mention her next requirement, afraid his temper would erupt again. But it was her money, and she should be able to handle it her way. "I'd also like a 'play' money fund."

Matt's brow wrinkled. " 'Play' money? Like in Monopoly?"

Tori smiled. "Kinda. I want to have an account that I can easily access for anything I want. I new dress. A short vacation. Sort of like a lot of pocket money. Instead of using a credit card all the time."

"Sounds like a good idea, actually," he said.

"I'm glad you think so because this is really important to me."

While he jotted some notes, she absently flipped the papers in front of her with her thumb. The moment he'd dropped the covers of the folder into place, something in her brain switched from business to personal. Although he'd been sitting beside her the last twenty or so minutes, she hadn't smelled his aftershave. Now it filled her senses so that she couldn't breathe anything else.

Had he been quite so close before? Of course he had. Only now she was aware that his bare arm brushed against hers when he reached forward to put his notebook on his desk.

"More soda?" he asked.

She nodded. "Yes. I'm so warm." She picked up the folder and fanned herself with it.

Matt, running his index finger inside his tight collar, knew what she was talking about. The heat was almost more than he could stand. But it wasn't a heat that could be cooled down by sipping an icy drink or loosening his tie. "Yes, I guess it is a little warm in here. I'll check the thermometer," Knowing that wouldn't help.

He refilled her glass and handed it to her. Their fingers brushed, and it was like being licked by fire.

"I have concert tickets for Saturday night," he said. "Will you go with me?"

Saturday night! Tori thought with dismay. All

or nothing. Feast or famine. She already had a date with Dain for Saturday night. Why couldn't anything ever work out right?

Dain's beach party promised to be fun. If today was any indication, Matt's company promised to be nothing less than provocative. What should she do?

Chapter Six

"A rock concert?" Tori asked eagerly.

She'd never been to a rock concert. When she was a teenager, her friends had gone to see almost every band that performed in Minneapolis, but her parents hadn't let her go with them. After a while, the other kids didn't bother inviting her anymore. As a result, she always felt left out and a little different. Now, finally, she had a chance to experience one of the things that had been missing from her life.

"Absolutely not." Matt laughed. "I'm too old to subject myself to ear-splitting guitar music and shouting singers. I had my fill when I was a kid. No. It's one of those summer pops things, where the orchestra plays show tunes and light opera. I've heard them perform before. They're very good. How about it?"

Enthusiasm for a rock concert had really excited Tori, now she felt let down. Nevertheless, no matter what entertainment Matt might have planned for them, an evening in his company would have been nice. But she'd already accepted Dain's offer, and she was too well brought-up to break a date with one man for another.

She looked at Matt through lowered lashes, remembering another time he'd invited her to lunch, just before she'd sold the house. Thinking he was merely being polite, she hadn't taken him seriously. Had he really meant to ask her for a date? Naa. Men like Matt Claussen didn't date mousy women like Victoria Gordon. Classy blondes like Tori Gordon were the type who caught their eye.

"Sorry," Tori said a bit regretfully. "I have plans for Saturday. Maybe some other time."

He curved his arm across the back of her chair and dangled his fingers lightly on her shoulder. "Cancel your date with Becker."

Her shoulder edged just out of his reach when she shrugged. "What makes you think it's with Dain? Maybe it's with someone else."

"I know." He inched closer so that once again his fingers brushed her sleeve. His voice lowered to a seductive pitch. "Wouldn't you rather spend the evening with me?"

"I've already made a commitment. You wouldn't want me to go back on my commitment, would you?"

"With him?" Matt put his free hand on his chest. "For me? Sure."

"Well, I wouldn't break a date with you for him, and I won't break a date with him for you." Fleetingly, she wondered if there was a way she could juggle both activities. Go to the concert first, then to the party later. It wouldn't be the first time something like that had been done, just the first time for her. But it was too late for that; she'd already told Matt she had a date.

"I'm sorry, Matt. I really can't. Please understand and give me a rain check, huh? Besides, I've been to pop concerts. I'd like to do something different. Something fun. Maybe we can go dancing sometime."

One of Matt's dark eyebrows shot up at the mention of the word fun. "Maybe," he said, "I do understand. But be careful. That . . . Becker considers himself a stud. You don't want to get in over your head."

"Don't worry, Matt. I can swim."

"Be careful anyway. The waters you're tackling have a very strong undertow."

"Thanks for the advice." She glanced at her watch. "Time to go."

As she put the folder into her briefcase, her high full breasts strained against the soft fabric of her blouse. Matt's lungs hurt as he struggled for breath. How could he let her leave now?

It was nearing evening. He could ask her if she'd like to have dinner with him. But he decided against it. He didn't think his ego could take another rebuff.

"I'll walk out with you," he said. "There's something in my car I want to give you."

When they stepped outside, he took her arm and led her toward an underground garage. "Would you like me to drive you to your car?" Anything to keep her with him a little longer.

She shook her head and smiled. "No thanks. It's right over there." She pointed to her BMW, baking in the setting sun. "What do you have for me?"

"Just some papers. But you might as well look them over while you're studying the other stuff."

"Okay." She felt disappointed. What had she been expecting?

She checked her new watch again. It was almost dinner time. Maybe, she hoped, he would invite her to join him for the meal. After she'd turned down his concert invitation, though, he was probably finished with her. She could ask him. The new Tori would. But she couldn't muster enough courage. Not yet. Maybe some other time when she was more comfortable in her new persona.

They came to his Cadillac and she stepped beside him just as he unlocked the trunk. As it popped up, he grabbed it, allowing it to open just wide enough for him to stick his hand in and take out a manila envelope. Just before he slammed the hood down, she glimpsed a white cowboy hat on the trunk floor. Aha, she thought.

He gave her the envelope and she linked her arm through his, gazing up at him. "Yours?"

Her eyes were wide and filled with innocence.

"My what?" Now his goose was cooked, Matt thought. He'd forgotten he'd tossed the hat into the trunk after leaving the pancake restaurant that morning. Thank goodness he'd admitted to owning one.

"That white ten-gallon hat," she crooned. "Seems I've seen it before somewhere."

"Seen one, seen them all." He led them back into the sunshine and shaded his face with his hand. "With my complexion, I burn very easily. I keep the hat close in case I find myself out in the sun."

She quirked an eyebrow. His skin was tanned as brown as the bark of the royal poinciana trees in the nearby park. The man would have to spend a whole day in the sun before he'd burn.

She suggested, "Or you might require it in case you need to go somewhere incognito."

"Why would I do that? I have nothing to hide."

His remark was so outrageous, he had to realize she knew he was lying in his teeth. Tori had two choices: either call him on it, or play along and treat it as a joke.

They came up to her car, and she said, "Well, Cowboy Matt, keep that hat handy. It's going to be a very sunny summer." She slid inside.

Grinning, he touched his forehead and replied, "Yes, ma'am." He slammed the door and backed away.

With a jaunty wave, she edged into the traffic that was streaming toward the bridge and West Palm Beach.

Dain tossed the prospectus for his magazine scheme on Tori's desk. She scanned it, liked the parts of it she understood, made some notes for Matt, then called him about it.

"Put it in the mail, please. I can't stop by. I'm tied up for the rest of the week."

"Okay," Tori said, feeling a bit hurt by his rebuff.

At first he'd rushed her, literally waiting on her doorstep, horning in on her dates. Now he didn't even want to see her. Was it because he'd gotten what he wanted from her—her investment business? Or had he been discouraged by her refusal to go out with him? Whatever the reason, they'd have to see each other soon because her money was still in the bank, not earning enough interest to suit Matt.

The moment Tori replaced the receiver, Irene buzzed her with a call from a client. For the rest of the day she was kept too busy to worry about Matt.

As soon as her ads for the house in Boca Raton had been published, there'd been an encouraging response, and she made several appointments to take prospective buyers to see the property. She also listed two more expensive homes, one in Boca, another in Palm Beach.

She was enthusiastic about the prospects, and excited over her successes.

And she wanted to share her good news with Matt. During the week, each time she called his office, his secretary told her he was either out of the office or with a client. Then he was out of town. He wouldn't get back to her before Monday.

If he knew he would be out of town all weekend, why had he asked her out for Saturday? Convinced he was playing some sort of cat-and-mouse game, she vowed not to call him again. Nor would she wait by the phone for him to call her. Didn't she prefer Dain's good-time company to Matt's, anyway?

Wendy plopped herself into the client's chair beside Tori's desk. "I like that new listing you have in Palm Beach." She tossed her head back, letting her golden hair cascade down her back. "I'm showing it this afternoon."

"Good," Tori declared. The last person she wanted to share a commission with was Wendy, but a sale by her was better than no sale at all.

"You don't mind?" Wendy twisted her index fingers around each other. Her red-tipped nails looked like blood on the talons of a vulture.

Of course Tori minded. "Why should I?" she asked sweetly. "The sooner the house is sold, the sooner I put more money in the bank."

"I don't envy you at tax time."

"Ah, but the rest of the year is heavenly. All

those shops. And vacations. I've already talked to a travel agent." Tori was fibbing, but Wendy's tight-lipped reaction was worth the white lie.

Wendy stood up saying, "I hope you have a wonderful time." Which Tori translated to mean *I hope you get a third degree sunburn and Montezuma's revenge.*

Lowering her head so that Wendy couldn't see her smug smile although feeling mean-spirited because of it, Tori idly looked at the photos of her newest listing. No matter what Tori said or did, the only thing that would even the score with Wendy for all those hurtful things she said about her in the rest room would be to admit that those cruel words had given her the push to change her image. Of course, she wouldn't have been able to afford to become Tori if it weren't for all the money she'd earned. She truly believed selling that one house had turned her life around forever.

Which brought her back to the photos. The more houses she sold, the more money she'd earn — and the more fun she'd have with the proceeds.

Wendy started to move away, then said, "Have you heard that I'm going out with Matt Claussen Saturday night? We're going to a concert. I'm so thrilled that he asked me."

Tori clenched her teeth. "I hope you have a wonderful time." Which translated to *I hope the concert is dull as nails and that you fall asleep and snore.*

Fighting jealousy she knew she shouldn't feel, Tori reminded herself that Matt had asked her to the concert first. If he wanted to spend an evening with that malicious woman, she had no more right to object than he had to tell her not to see Dain. Supposedly, Matt was out of town. Which of them, she wondered, was lying? Given Matt's history of honesty, there wasn't much doubt. She glared at Wendy.

Saturday evening, as Tori sorted through her bathing suits, trying to choose one suitable for the beach party, she wondered if Matt would go for the hat trick and intrude in her third date with Dain. Even if he wanted to, how would he know where to find the party? Beaches extended along the Atlantic coast for miles and miles.

No. She needn't worry that he'd ruin things for her this time. Besides, he was out of town — or he was with Wendy, depending on whom she wanted to believe.

Holding up a black one-piece French-cut bathing suit, she decided it was perfect. Low cut and figure-hugging, it couldn't be considered conservative, yet it wasn't sexy enough to give Dain the wrong idea. After she slipped it on, she pulled a V-necked sleeveless cotton shift over her head.

She smoothed on blusher and a tinge of violet eye shadow then spread red, red lipstick on her lips. For a while, she fiddled with her hair, unable to decide on a style that would keep it relatively clean and out of her eyes while at the same time being chic. In the end, she twisted it into a French braid. Although she'd sometimes worn it that way when it was mousy brown, she thought the golden braid looked rather jaunty. Satisfied with her reflection in the full-length mirror on the back of her bathroom door, she stepped into new, expensive sandals, stuffed a few necessities into a tote bag, grabbed her keys, and left the condo.

The party, Dain had told her, was to start around seven o'clock. He planned to be there early because he was bringing the beer, so she could come anytime she liked. When she heard that, she felt sorry she'd decided against going to the concert with Matt and then attending the party fashionably late. Dain was so wishy-washy about the whole thing, she wondered if he really wanted her to come.

But what Dain wanted wasn't the issue. What she wanted was what counted. And she, Tori Gordon, wanted to have fun. By her standards, she was rich and the time had come to really celebrate her success. She'd let her hair down literally and figuratively. Now she was finally going to enjoy her life.

Dain's directions were perfect; when she parked her car, it was just after seven o'clock. Where the sand met the asphalt of the parking lot, she began to remove her sandals and put them into her tote bag. She stepped onto the beach and her toes curled into the warm, yielding sand that still retained the sun's warmth.

Overhead, the sky was aflame with every shade of red from light pink to deep magenta. Seabirds swooped into the pink-tinged ocean for a last meal before roosting for the night. She inhaled deeply. The air was warm and, oh, so sweet.

She scanned the sandy expanse for signs of the party and heard the music before she located a group setting up a table near the waterline. She hoped the tide was in, because if it wasn't, they'd have to move again before long. She picked her way toward them, careful of broken shells and debris.

When she spotted Dain, she waved. The skimpy white swim trunks he wore left little to the imagination. His well-defined chest muscles attested to many hours in a health club. His hips were narrow, and his flat stomach was lightly furred with dark hair that disappeared into the almost nonexistent strip of fabric that passed for bathing trunks. To her surprise and disappointment, she found his polished machismo intimidating and not at all appealing.

"Hi." He hugged her and would have given her a lingering kiss if she hadn't gently pulled away.

"Hi," she replied, locking her eyes on his face, too uncomfortable to look anywhere else.

He put his hand on her back. "Party has already started. But when the sun goes down it'll really get going."

"Our hostess." Dain introduced Tori to a red-headed woman arranging covered serving dishes on the table.

Then he led her a little further down the beach. "This is our blanket," he said, dropping onto a quilt. "Take off that cover-up thing and get comfortable."

Dain watched her intently as she pulled her shift over her head. She felt as if she were stripping for him, and a spasm of awkwardness made her movements clumsy. Thank goodness she'd chosen to wear the conservative bathing suit. Not conservative, she admonished herself. Never conservative. It was understated.

Dain whistled. "That's some figure you were hiding under those baggy business suits. I can't believe how blind I was, but my eyes are open now." He reached up and took her hand. "Sit down. Here. Beside me."

He gave a tug. To her dismay, she lost her balance and tumbled on top of him. Before she could scramble away, he grabbed her and planted a hot, wet kiss full on her mouth.

She smacked her hands against his chest, feeling the springy hairs and flexing muscles beneath her fingers. She pushed. Hard. Instead of releasing her, he toppled over, pulling her with him. Immediately, their arms and legs tangled, and their bodies pressed intimately together. Too intimately. With all her strength, she levered herself off him and jumped to her feet.

Tugging the elastic around the leg of her bathing suit, she said, "Let's go swimming."

He shook his head. "This is better." He lunged for her.

Lithely she sidestepped and evaded him. "I'm going swimming," she insisted. "Coming?"

She began running toward the surf. When she glanced back, Dain was slowly getting to his feet. Just as slowly, he followed her into the warm, calm ocean.

During the next few hours Tori saw little of Dain. Each time she chanced to spot him, he was with a different woman—talking, dancing, kissing. Not that she cared; she was having a wonderful time mingling with some of the other guests—a couple of musicians, a magazine writer, a painter, an Irishman who had sailed the Atlantic alone, and a dog breeder. She chatted with them all.

For a while she danced to rock music booming from a tape player. Heavy metal gave way to the beat of the limbo, and from out of nowhere a broomstick appeared. A line of partygoers formed and there was much laughter and applause as, one by one, they tried to duck beneath the ever-lowering stick. On her last try Tori fell and she lay giggling helplessly, spreadeagled like a starfish on the yellow sand.

117

Now the music took on a Latin beat and soon a congo line was snaking along the beach, with Tori somewhere in the middle, hanging on to the jerking hips of the Irish sailor. Finally she gave up, laughing and out of breath. By now, the evening breeze was cool, so she slipped her cotton cover-up over her head before joining Dain, who was sitting with three other realtors, talking shop.

As she dropped crosslegged onto the blanket, one of them, a dark-haired woman in her early forties wearing three or four rings said, "So you're the lady who sold the Palmworth mansion. I'm impressed."

"So am I." Ellis Clayborne, Dain's friend who wanted to start the real estate publication, draped a thin arm around Tori's shoulder. "Tell us your secret."

"No. secret. Just a question of finding the right customer."

"You make it sound so easy," said the third realtor, a lush redhead in a green bikini and an amber necklace.

Tori had never been the center of attention before, and she was flattered by their compliments, loving every minute of it.

Ellis took his arm from her shoulder and patted her knee. "That's because she's so good." He took his hand away before she could move.

She grinned at him, torn between his unwelcome familiarity and his flattery. "Thanks."

If only Matt were here to listen to them fawning over her. He wouldn't be so quick to put down Dain and his friends. Thinking of Matt for at least the hundredth time that evening, she looked around for him. He'd probably been at that damned concert with Wendy. By now the concert had to be over. If he was going to make an appearance, it would be soon.

Just then, she spotted a cowboy hat, head and shoulders above a crowd that had gathered around the guitar strummers.

"Excuse me," she said, rising to her feet in one graceful motion. "I want to get something to drink."

"Bring me back a beer, will you," Dain said.

"Sure."

She trudged to the coolers, took out two tepid cans, and made for the cowboy hat. Her heart beating in rhythm to the frenetic music, she elbowed her way into the circle. That man was going to get a piece of her mind!

Coming up behind him, she saw that his arm was circling the waist of a blonde. Jealousy brushed aside her anger. How could he be so cruel? Bad enough to come to the party to check up on her. Worse to bring Wendy with him.

She edged closer and grasped his arm.

"Hey!"

He wasn't Matt.

Cowboy pulled his arm away and turned around. The surprised expression on the stranger's face changed to friendly warmth when he saw her. "Well, hi, little lady." He tipped the brim of his hat. "What can I do for you?"

Embarrassment flushed her face. "I'm sorry. I thought you were someone else."

"That's okay, little lady. You got me now."

Tori backed away. "Sorry," she repeated and tried to melt into the crowd.

Pressing a can on each of her hot cheeks, she ran back to Dain's blanket. Only Dain and Ellis remained there.

"I hear you're interested in investing in our little project," Ellis said.

"Yes, I am. I sent your prospectus to my financial advisor. I should have a decision sometime next week."

Ellis patted her knee again, and she shrank away, telling herself he was just being friendly. If she wanted to have fun, she'd have to relax and not be such a prude.

"I guarantee you won't be sorry if you decide to invest with us," Ellis said.

"Not only do I want to invest with you, but I can't wait to advertise in the magazine. I think it's a wonderful concept." Putting the can of beer to her lips, she tilted her head back and took a sip. The brew had become warm and tasted bland and flat.

The crowd was thinning, Tori noticed. Couples were either drifting away, seeking privacy, or heading toward the parking lot. She didn't want to be alone with Dain on a secluded beach and was glad she'd brought her own car.

Over his protestations, she gathered up her belongings and after a quick thank you to her hostess, headed for the parking lot. To her surprise, the glowing digits of the car clock showed it was almost one o'clock. How quickly the time had passed when she was having a really good time. She smiled into the darkness. It had been just the kind of fun evening she'd dreamed about.

Tori arrived home tired, looking forward to a warm shower and bed. The light on the answering machine in the living room was flashing, and she switched the button to messages.

Matt's voice, distorted by the tape, rasped: "Tori. It's about seven-thirty, Saturday. Sorry I missed you. Call me as soon as you get home. I don't care how late. It's important."

The man had some nerve. He'd snubbed her all week, now he wanted to hear from her ASAP. No way would she call him tonight. Let him stew till morning. Let him think she'd spent the night with Dain. Besides, wasn't he out with Wendy? Did he want her to call just to talk to his answering machine?

By the time she came out of the shower, hair dripping wet, a towel draped around the collar of her robe, curiosity had gotten the better of her. What could be so important that he'd want her to call no matter when? She dialed his number.

His voice, when he answered, was groggy. "Tori! What time is it?"

"You said in your message that time didn't matter."

"It doesn't."

"Sorry I woke you." Closing her eyes, she visualized him in his bed, his hair tousled from sleep. His body naked beneath a light blanket. Or did he use a blanket? Her eyes snapped open. Was he alone?

"It's okay," he said, sounding more alert. "I needed to talk to you—needed to hear your voice. I wasn't able to get back to you all week because I was out of town."

"Oh?" Likely story. "That's what your secretary said." She wedged the phone between her cheek and shoulder to free her hands to towel dry her hair.

"I had to fly out to California. My father had a mild heart attack."

She dropped the towel and grasped the receiver. "Oh! I'm sorry." Was he telling her the truth? Certainly he wouldn't lie about his father's health. "I hope he's okay."

"He'll be fine if he stops smoking."

"And he won't?"

"Maybe now he will. He'd better. Even though I love him, I can't seem to get over being angry with him. He knew what those damned cigarettes were doing to him!"

"I understand how you feel, Matt. But you have to realize that the ultimate choice is his. It's an old habit that's awfully hard to break."

"I know. I know." With those simple words, his worry and frustration came through to her. Then he changed the subject by asking, "Did you have a good time tonight?"

"Yes. As a matter of fact, I did. How about you? Did you get back in time for the concert?"

"I didn't plan to go. When you said you wouldn't go with me, I gave the tickets to Wendy Neff."

"Gave them to her?" Ah, Tori thought Wendy was the one who was lying. That was no surprise.

"No point having them go to waste. Victoria?"

"Tori. Hum?"

"Can I see you tomorrow?"

"Well . . . I . . . ." Her ambivalence toward him was going to drive her crazy. She wanted to see him, had missed him in fact, but he was so . . . so serious-minded. If only they'd gotten together before she'd worked so hard to change her image. His no-nonsense personality suited Victoria's stodgy attitude perfectly. "What did you have in mind?"

"A beach party of our own. We'll pack a lunch. Catch up on our tans. Or have you had your fill of sand and surf?"

"No, not at all. It sounds delightful." Quiet but pleasant, she thought. She could use a restful day after tonight's frantic pace. "What time should I meet you?"

"Meet? I'll pick you up around eleven. I'll bring the food, you bring the sunscreen."

"Okay. See you tomorrow. Or, rather, today."

"Sleep well, Victoria. Dream of me."

"Tori," she said to the dial tone. *Will that man ever call me Tori?*

In the morning she woke to the boom of thunder and the rat-a-tat of rain hammering against her window. Her first thought was that her date with Matt would be ruined. She pressed her lips together. Maybe it was for the best. She didn't need him complicating her life. She didn't need to spend her nights dreaming about him.

She was pouring herself a cup of coffee when the phone rang.

It was Matt. "We can't go to the beach."

"Probably not," she replied. "I listened to the weather report. They predicted it'll rain like this all day. We can try again next week."

"That's fine, but what do you want to do today? We shouldn't let a little rain spoil our fun."

A little rain? Rain sheeted across her window so thick she couldn't see through it. "I don't know. How about a movie?"

"Naa. Can't you think of something more exciting? A museum?"

She laughed. "That's exciting?"

"Guess not." There was a pause. "I've got an idea. Dress casual. I'll be over at eleven." He hung up.

Intrigued, she pulled on purple knit leggings and an oversized striped purple and white T-shirt. She brushed her hair and left it loose to ripple down her back, then dabbed White Diamonds on her pulse points.

At exactly eleven o'clock, Matt rang the doorbell. He carried a large wicker basket, and a plaid blanket was draped over his arm. He grinned. "If the couple can't go to the picnic, the picnic will come to the couple."

He wore nothing but a pair of tan bathing trunks and rubber beach shoes. Rain dripped off his hair and skin onto the tile floor. He couldn't have been wetter if he'd just come out of the ocean.

Tori put her hands on her hips and laughed. "Didn't want to ruin your clothes in the rain?"

"Since this is supposed to be a beach party, I might as well be wet."

As he crossed the small entryway to put the basket on the breakfast nook, she cocked her head and studied his body. Although not quite as muscular as Dain, Matt was solid and well built and infinitely more appealing. At that moment, she was consumed with the desire to touch him.

Instead, she took a clean dishtowel from a drawer and tossed it to him.

Catching it easily, he rubbed it over his face and hair, then dropped it on the tile counter. "I left something in the car. I'll be right back."

"The cowboy hat?" she quipped.

A grin was his answer. While he was gone, she wondered what he would surprise her with next. His mystery picnic was getting better and better. She was peeking into the wicker basket when he returned, and she dropped the lid as if she'd been caught with her hand in the cookie jar.

She whirled around and started laughing when she saw he was carrying a vinyl blow-up palm tree almost as tall as he was.

"Can't have a beach party without a palm tree," he said.

"Did you bring the ocean with you, too."

Grinning, he shook his head and splattered her with raindrops. "Not the ocean, but a lot of water." He set the tree in a corner.

Was this the same staid Matt Claussen? "I suppose that's our lunch in the basket?"

"Yup. And this." He reached into the basket and pulled out a video tape. "Here." He handed it to her. "You get this started while I spread the blanket."

When she read the title on the spine of the tape case, she guffawed. "You're kidding, right? *Beach Blanket Bingo?*"

"No. Not kidding." He pushed the coffee table out of the way, flapped the blanket, and spread it in front of the television set. "It's to get us in the mood."

"In the mood for what?" The tape snapped

easily into the machine.

"We planned to spend the day at the beach. This is our beach."

Kicking off his shoes, he dropped onto the blanket and leaned back against the bottom of the sofa. "Start the movie."

She pushed the play button on the VCR and sat down crosslegged near the edge of the blanket, keeping her spine ramrod straight.

"I won't bite."

"What?"

"You don't have to sit like a Sunday school teacher. Lean back. Come here next to me." He moved over a couple of inches to make more room for her. "I'm really a perfect gentleman."

Why, he wondered, was Victoria so skittish around him? If she wasn't afraid to go out with The Jerk, she certainly had no reason to worry about being alone with him.

Slowly, she scooted on her behind until her back was against the sofa, but at least a foot of space separated them. Her sweet scent wafted across the short distance and found its way into his heart. A stirring in his groin took his mind away from the movie, but he forced his eyes to focus on the screen. Not a minute earlier, he'd told her he was a gentleman. Now he had to live up to it.

Chapter Seven

"Uncle." Tori threw up her hands in surrender. Startled, Matt jumped. "What?"

"I cry uncle. I give up. This is the silliest movie I've ever seen."

She leaned over on her knees to switch off the VCR, offering him an enticing view of her derriere. Outlined beneath the thin knit of her stretch pants was the soft curve that made Matt's palms itch to touch. He bent his fingers and scratched the palms without receiving the least bit of satisfaction.

"Hope you don't mind, but I've really had enough." She rocked back to a sitting position, and a tendril of hair drifted across her face.

"Mind?" Mind that she'd removed the tantalizing vision from his sight? Damned right he minded.

He sat so close to her that when he blew out a puff of air, it stirred wisps of her hair. His hand reached out as if it had a will of its own and brushed a curl back behind her ear, deliberately grazing the sensitive shell. Did she have any idea what she was doing to him?

"I missed you," he said. This past week without Victoria had seemed the longest of his life. Even though he'd been with his family, he'd felt alone. She'd have provided the anchor he'd needed so badly. But it was too soon, way too soon.

"You did?"

He nodded. "Did you miss me?" His hand came to rest on the side of her neck.

"Well. Maybe a little." Tori bent her head and gave him easier access to her sensitized skin.

"I checked my messages when I got back. You called quite a few times." His words were prosaic, but his voice crooned a golden refrain.

"I listed two more houses." If only he would stop touching her that way . . . She cleared her throat. "I wanted to tell you about it."

"Congratulations." His index finger skimmed her earlobe and his pinkie nestled in the hollow of her throat. "We should celebrate."

Every place he touched sparked on her skin. Her heart began to race. "Thanks. I think . . . I think. . . ." But she couldn't think. She could barely breathe.

With gentle pressure, he brought her face toward him. His lips teased hers, then brushed her cheek in a feathery caress. Strong arms wrapped around her. The awkward way they were sitting on the blanket left her no choice but to shuffle around until she nestled half on his lap.

She reached up to touch his jaw and felt the strength of his rapidly throbbing pulse. His life-blood was racing because of her! Infused with the exhilaration of her power over him, she wove her fingers in his thick hair, urging his mouth back to hers. Her senses swam with his citrusy aftershave.

"Matt," she murmured.

Needing little encouragement, he increased the pressure on her lips. The tip of his tongue flicked on her teeth. She parted them, presenting him with the damp warmth of her mouth like a flower opening to a honeybee.

"Ah, Victoria," he whispered.

For the first time, she didn't correct his misuse of her name. It had become a caress as arousing as his touch. With just two words he had spliced her life force with his.

He tightened his arms around her until he felt the thrust of her hardened nipples against his bare chest. The small moan that came from her throat was an erotic response that merely whet-ted his hunger. He ached. Her arms grazing the nakedness of his chest and back gave him a small, incendiary sampling of what her touch could do to him.

His desire for her was as primal as his need for breath. He hungered for her as a starving man craves sustenance.

His fingers found their way beneath the hem

of her T-shirt. The warmth from her silky skin as his palms traced the ridges of her spine challenged his control.

Instinct warned that he could take her only so far without jeopardizing the tenuous ties of their budding relationship. He wouldn't push her. But court her slowly. Tantalize her until she was ready for him to bring her to the heights of their passion. Not today perhaps, but the day would come—soon. Until then, he would savor every delicious moment he held her.

"You fit just right in my arms," he said, gliding his hands down her sides to measure the span of her waist.

When he came to the boundary of her waistband, he paused in his mission of discovery, then retraced his trail upward until he felt the lower limit of her bra. He splayed his hands across her rib cage, daring to go no further.

Their tongues wrapped around each other, exploring rough textures and smooth. Nothing Tori had ever experienced had prepared her for the overwhelming sensations swaying through her body. Hot and hotter. Strong and stronger. Desire threatened to vanquish her being.

She felt his need against her hip. Her own moist, burning hunger matched his. She wanted to tell him something, but there were no words, only hands and fingers, mouths and tongues.

Beneath it all, the tiniest bit of good sense still remained, warning her it was too soon, that she wasn't ready for Matt to be in her life that way.

There was a reason, she knew, but what it was, she couldn't remember. Not while her body pulsed with life beneath Matt's touch. Not while Matt was holding her, caressing her.

Easing her mouth off his, she scattered tiny kisses across his cheek, gently nipping his skin. Then she buried her face against the racing pulse in his throat and braced her hands on his shoulders. Matt knew the imprints left by her lips and fingers would last forever.

He understood the meaning of her subtle withdrawal. Reluctantly, slowly, he loosened his physical hold on her body and slackened his emotional coupling with her soul.

Tori slid off his leg and sat facing him. "Wow," she said, gasping for breath.

She brushed her hair from her face with trembling fingers. All of a sudden she became aware of the storm that whipped the wind through the palm fronds and slashed rain against the windows, just as the aftermath of his kisses whipped and slashed at her emotions.

"Yeah," he answered. "Wow." Unable to release her completely, he rested his fingers lightly on her wrist. "There's something between us, Victoria, hard as you try to fight it."

"I'm not fighting it." She jerked her hand away and jumped up. "Do you call what just happened fighting?"

He nodded, and slowly got to his feet. "If you weren't fighting it, we wouldn't be standing here now. We'd be—"

"Making love?" she finished for him.

"Would that be so bad?"

"No." She strode to the sliding glass door and yanked the cord that opened the slats on the vertical blinds. "But I'm not ready."

"I know." He stepped behind her.

She turned to face him. "You do?"

He nodded. "You've said it over and over, a hundred different ways."

"I didn't realize you understood. I thought that when I kissed you, when I — "

"Yeah, you kissed me," he said, frowning. "As wonderful as it was, I knew you were holding back." He cupped her cheek for a moment then moved away.

"I'm sorry, Matt. I. . . ." She reached out to him, then dropped her hand to her side.

He turned back. "It's okay. When you're ready, I'll know."

But she'd never be ready for him, she thought with a touch of wistfulness. Much as she was attracted to him, Matt Claussen wasn't the kind of man she needed. They'd argue about money and her choice of life-style until their relationship was destroyed. Besides, she didn't want a relationship — she wanted to have a good time before she settled down.

Sure she could make love with him. But what she wanted right now was to be free. And despite her desire to lead a fun-filled life, she wasn't the kind of woman who could fall into bed with a man and not make a commitment to him. One-night stands or casual affairs weren't for her.

Tori turned back to the window and watched the rain splash into pond-size puddles on the lawn. At least the ducks must be happy, she thought.

"Are you ready for lunch?" Matt asked.

Surprised at the abrupt change in subject, she glanced over her shoulder. When her eyes fell on him, her heart skipped a beat, then raced to catch up. He had pulled on a button-down T-shirt and was running his hand around the collar to straighten it, but his hair still stood up where she'd pulled her fingers through it. Her fingertips tingled with the desire to wipe off the faint streak of plum-colored lipstick which brightened his cheekbone, while her lips yearned to add a matching stripe to the other cheek.

Lunch? Could she really eat? Her appetite hungered for other things. "I guess so. Sure."

"Go sit down," he said. "I'll get the food."

Tori sank down in the middle of the blanket. Resting her chin on her bent knees, she watched him dig into the picnic hamper. From its depths he pulled out foil-wrapped containers and set them on the breakfast bar. He removed plates, silverware, a linen tablecloth and napkins, and two stem glasses from the fitted lid.

Finally, he took out a bottle of wine and held it up. With a sheepish grin, he said, "Whoops. I forgot to put it back in the refrigerator. But it's still pretty cold. I think it'll be okay."

"I'm sure it will," she said and jumped up again. She was as squirrely as a two-year-old. "I'll set the table." She started to stack the silverware atop the plates.

"No!"

Surprised at his vehemence, she dropped a fork. Matt and she bent to pick it up at the same time. Her breast brushed against his bare thigh, sending a tremor of pure delight through her. Her balance already off-kilter, she almost toppled over. He steadied her with a hand on her back, which did nothing to calm her screaming nerve endings.

Finally, Matt snagged the fork. Without bothering to rinse it off, he put it on top of the plates.

"This is a picnic," he explained. "Picnics must be eaten on blankets. It's the law."

"Oh. Well, I certainly don't want the picnic police to raid us," she said with a still shaky voice. "The neighbors would never stop talking." Because his touch had left her knees trembling, she perched on a stool at the breakfast bar. Propping her elbows on the tile, she rested her chin on her interlaced fingers and watched him. "Why don't we just leave the food on the counter and fill our plates from here."

"Good plan." He eased the cork out of the wine bottle, decanted some into each glass, and handed her one.

Holding it up, she clinked it against his. "To a successful business relationship."

"To good . . . friends."

She wished she could read his mind. The expression in his eyes was so intent that she knew without a doubt that the short pause meant more than the words.

While she watched him unpack the food, she sipped the smooth dry wine. She expected to see the old picnic standbys of cold chicken and coleslaw, but the first package he brought out overflowed with fried rice.

"I have to reheat this," he said, putting the cardboard container into the microwave.

Then he peeled back the wrapping on an oblong dish to reveal white circles about an inch in diameter with something blackish in the middle. Sushi! Now *that* was a surprise. Little by little, Mr. Claussen was chipping away at her original impression of him. Unfortunately, she'd have to eat the stuff. Victoria wouldn't allow that raw fish in her mouth, but Tori would try anything—as long as it wasn't fried grasshoppers. She sighed, wondering if Victoria hadn't had the right idea after all.

"I've never eaten sushi," she stammered.

"What? You've never tried the yuppie equivalent to fish sticks? I'm surprised. The J—I mean Becker is slipping."

"I'm sure he'd have gotten around to it," she commented dryly.

"Well, I'm glad I got there first."

She had the distinct impression they weren't

talking about raw fish. "How do you eat it—the sushi?"

"Just pop it in your mouth. Chew a few times then swallow." He picked up a piece and put it to her lips.

For a moment, she pressed her teeth together. Then she remembered that Tori Gordon was game to try anything. She opened her mouth and he popped in the morsel. As he withdrew his hand, she nicked the tip of his finger with her tongue.

Taking the opportunity to run his thumb along her bottom lip, he advised, "Now you're supposed to chew."

Her lungs were like airtight chambers. He had to stop touching her like that! She couldn't chew. Nor could she swallow.

"Chew!"

She obeyed.

It tasted a little fishy but bland. Its starch consistency made it difficult to get down her throat.

"Enough. Are you going to spit it out or what?"

She swallowed.

"Good." She forced enthusiasm while she tried to clear her tongue of the gooey stuff.

"Uh huh," was his only comment before he unwrapped another container. Tori saw mixed greens in the bowl and sighed with relief before she noticed something tan in the salad. She shuddered, imagining what gastronomic horrors it might be.

"Chinese chicken salad," he explained. "What picnic would be complete without chicken?"

So it was chicken, huh? Could she believe him, or was he trying to sneak octopus or tripe or something even more exotic onto her unsophisticated palate? She wrinkled her brow. She had no reason to doubt him. If anything, he was always honest with her.

The microwave beeped, and he retrieved the rice, putting it beside the other containers on the countertop. "It's ready." He pointed. "You go first."

While she filled her plate with salad, rice, and just a couple of pieces of sushi, Matt shook out the tablecloth and spread it on the blanket. The inflated palm tree toppled over, and he righted it, setting it beside the sofa so that its make-believe shade would protect them from the make-believe sun.

Sitting down on the blanket again, she balanced her food and the wineglass on the lumpy cloth. Crosslegged beside her, Matt tried to balance the plate on his knee while eating, but it kept dipping, and he had to grab for it. The palm tree fell over and clunked him on the head. "This is a little awkward, isn't it?" he said as he pushed the tree off while somehow managing to keep the contents from slipping off his plate.

"Yeah. A little." She laughed. "Most picnickers just have to worry about ants. We have to cope with palm trees." She leaned across his legs to help straighten the dangerously tilting tree. "It would have been easier if we'd eaten at the table."

"But not as much fun," he said, pulling her against him. He stole a kiss before the tree knocked him on the head again. "This thing sure has it in for me," he said, pushing it off him while she sat back where she belonged.

With the tree safely out of the way, lying on its side like felled timber, he picked up his plate. "So tell me about those houses you listed."

Tori described the two new houses she'd added to her roster. "They're both huge." She spread her arms wide apart. "One even has an indoor lap pool besides the regulation kidney-shaped one. The other has ten bedrooms. And that's not counting the guest house." She went on to tell him about the interested buyers who'd made appointments to see them. "You'd think Sunday would be the busiest time for me. But all these people are out-of-towners and are coming in next week — after a stop in Disney World, of course."

"Of course. Well, I hope they're legitimate buyers, not looky loos."

"They may not buy, but I think they're seriously looking." She crossed her fingers. "I hope they buy."

"I hope so, too, Victoria. Want some more sushi?"

"No thanks. Why don't you —"

"Chicken salad?"

"Okay." Giving up the attempt to have him

call her Tori, she handed him her plate. "And some fried rice."

When he brought it back, a fried chicken wing and a leg were perched atop the rice.

"What's this?" she asked, tearing the wing apart. She was never so happy to see chicken in her life.

"Backup. In case you didn't like the sushi."

"Was it that obvious?"

"Uh-huh. You kept looking at it as if it were something I'd scraped off the bottom of my shoe instead of something I paid top dollar for."

"Top dollar, huh?" She picked up the wing and took a big bite. With her mouth full, she said, "Now this is good and worth every penny."

"So is sushi. If you like it. Obviously, it's not for everyone."

"Do you like it?"

"Yeah. But I'm a Californian. We're supposed to like stuff like that."

"And speaking of California," she said, before taking another bite, "how's your father doing?"

"Pretty good, or I wouldn't have left. He's already home from the hospital. The attack was a warning. I hope he takes it seriously."

"Will he?"

Matt shrugged. "Mom'll see that he does."

"Wives are like that."

Again, she saw that intent expression in his eyes. It burned into her, and she looked away, unwilling to learn what he was trying to tell her.

A few more bites and the bones were cleaned.

She ate the last of the rice then asked, "What's for dessert?"

"Dessert? I'm not sure. . . ." now his eyes twinkled.

"Stop teasing. You didn't put together this elaborate picnic and forget the dessert."

He lifted one shoulder. "I guess you're right." Standing up, he stacked their plates and took them back to the kitchen. "I brought dessert, but the logistics of coffee were beyond me. I thought of a Thermos, but that's so ordinary. And being the fun-loving kind of guy that I am, I wouldn't settle for something as mundane as a Thermos."

Matt? Fun-loving? She watched him over her shoulder. "Do you want coffee?" she asked. He was as serious-minded as the old Victoria. Hardworking. Considerate. Intelligent. But fun-loving? Hardly.

"Only if it's flavored."

"Flavored? The only coffee I have is coffee flavored. Take it or leave it."

"I'll leave it. I'd rather drink the wine, anyway."

"Me, too. What about the dessert? I'm dying to see what it is." Gooey sweet chocolate cake? "Did you bring back carrot cake from California? Or a New York cheesecake from the deli?" Or had he brought one slice of Key lime pie? Her lips prickled, reliving the intimacy of sharing that other slice.

"Not even close." He took out a big spoon

and scooped something out of a bowl onto dessert dishes.

The fluffy white stuff that jiggled on the dish he handed her was even more unfamiliar to her than sushi. She saw pieces of fruit and what looked like cake, but it was covered with a creamy concoction. "What is this?"

"Taste it."

"Not till you tell me what it is."

"Victoria, you're being conservative again. Give it a try."

"Tori," she mumbled. Why did she bother? Under his watchful eyes, she took a bite. Sweet and tart at the same time, it tasted heavenly.

"This is wonderful. What is it?"

"English trifle. A hodgepodge of rum-spiked cake, fruit, custard, jam, and whipped cream."

"It's delicious." Her tongue darted out to lick away a drop of cream from her lower lip. His attention focused on her mouth.

"I was so sure you'd like it, I didn't bother to bring a back-up."

"Who wouldn't like it?"

He leaned over and licked away another fleck of cream from her lip. Her eyes locked with his as he backed away.

"Thanks for the picnic, Matt. It's been . . . wonderful."

"And fun?"

Fun, as she'd come to understand it when she was on the outside looking in, was dancing the night away in a boisterous nightclub, or doing the limbo at a beach party, or sailing, or any number of other activities that called for physical exertion and other people with which to share it. In other words, all the activities that had been missing from her life until now.

But, yes, to her surprise, Matt's impromptu picnic-for-two had been fun.

"Absolutely. I'm having a wonderful time. Thanks, Matt."

"You're welcome. I'm enjoying it, too."

The sparkle in Victoria's eyes warmed Matt's heart. He had no choice but to dare another kiss. Her lips were warm and filled with promise, but when his tongue tried to urge them apart, she pulled back. He noticed that her fork rattled against the plate when she scooped up another bite of trifle.

After swallowing it, she said, "I've looked over all the papers you gave me, and signed them. Do you want them now?"

"Are you sure you want to take care of business today?"

"It's as good a time as any." She stood up. "As soon as we clear away the picnic."

As they put the dishes back into the hamper, Tori again marveled at serious Matt's light-hearted "beach party." Whoever would have thought that he would own a fitted picnic basket? He was the type who'd use a grocery bag then save it to recycle. There was nothing wrong with that, of course, but a picnic basket was so . . . so . . . romantic.

"It really was fun, Matt. Maybe . . . we'll do it again sometime."

"Absolutely. Next time at the real beach."

She nodded, then walked toward the dining room table and pointed to the folder he'd given her. "Everything's right here."

"I have some recommendations regarding Clayborne's project." He sat down. "I knew you wouldn't listen to me when I advised you not to get involved. So I've broken down the figures and come up with what I think would be a fair investment that won't hurt you when they go broke."

"You're such a pessimist. They're not going to go broke. They're going to get rich."

"If you say so," he said as he sorted through the papers she'd signed. "Everything seems to be in order."

He tore off the originals, and put her copies back into the folder and his into the wicker basket. "That should do it." He looked out the kitchen window. "It's stopped raining. Want to go for a walk?"

"Sure."

They put on their shoes and left the condo. Outside, water dripped from the trees and rushed along the curb like miniature raging rivers. But puffy white clouds powdered the blue sky, and the sun, lowering toward the horizon, was shining gloriously.

When Victoria started to walk away from the front stoop, Matt took her hand. He looked down at their ten intertwined fingers. Just as her body fit perfectly to his, their hands melded perfectly.

She hopped over a puddle. "Tell me about your family."

"There's just my two brothers and me. I'm in the middle."

"Nieces and nephews?" She swatted at an insect that buzzed in front of her face.

"Two of each. Preschoolers. They all live in Southern California.

"How about you? You told me you were from Minneapolis, but you didn't say much about your family."

"Mom and Dad still live in the house where they raised me and my brother and sister. I'm the youngest." Tori frowned and gazed out over the expanse of sodden lawn. "They're content to raise their families in the old neighborhood. Unfortunately, they can't seem to understand that I want something different. My brother's taking over Dad's plumbing business, and my sister is a homemaker."

Matt nodded in understanding. "They gave you a hard time when you wanted to move away, huh?"

"Did they ever. It's like we live on two different planets." The resentment rankled as if she'd experienced the hurts yesterday rather than four years ago. "Mom still can't understand why I didn't marry the boy next door."

"Why didn't you?"

"Because I didn't love him."

The fingers holding hers tightened. "If you loved him, would you have given up your dreams?"

She shook her head. "I don't think so." She felt the grip on her hand loosen a bit. "I wanted a career so badly I could taste it. I don't know where that drive came from. Maybe I needed to prove to my siblings that I could succeed. I was the youngest, and they were always putting me down. Whenever I wanted to accomplish something, they told me it was beyond my reach. So I guess in a way, I'm still trying to prove that baby sister is capable of setting goals and achieving them."

"You've certainly proved that you can succeed."

Facing him, she grinned. "Yeah, I guess I have."

"And what did they say when you told them?"

"I haven't."

Matt stopped short and stared at her incredulously. "You haven't told them? Why not?"

"I don't know." She shrugged.

When his expression turned to disbelief, she grimaced and said, "I'd rather imagine them proud of me than find out that they're not."

"That's defeatist thinking. Like figuring if you don't try, you can't fail." He was surprised at her. He'd always admired her take-charge attitude and never thought of her as a coward.

"Defeatist?" She considered the word. "Maybe

so. But I know the Gordons of Minnesota wouldn't understand how important that sale was to me."

"Then you either have to explain it to them so they do understand, or accept it and not let it get to you."

"It doesn't get to me. Not anymore."

"Hah!" he scoffed. He moved his hand to the small of her back. Exerting just a bit of pressure, he turned her around, and they started walking the way they'd come. "I think you should call your mother. When was the last time you spoke to her?"

"Last week."

"Last week! And you didn't tell her? Come on." He hurried her along. "We're going back so that you can make that phone call. Right now!"

She dragged her sandals through a puddle, getting her feet wet. "Not now, Matt. It's been a wonderful day. I don't want anything to spoil it."

"It won't." He hoped he wasn't wrong. He didn't know her family, could only trust his instincts about people he'd never met. "If they let you down, I'll be here with a strong shoulder to cry on. But I'll bet they won't disappoint you. As a matter of fact, I'm willing to put my money where my mouth is."

"Oh yeah?" Hands on hips, she saw the challenge and prepared herself for it.

"Yeah. If your parents aren't the proudest people in Minneapolis by the time you finish

147

telling them about your big sale, I'll buy you dinner tomorrow."

"Sounds good so far." She forced a tight-lipped smile. "What happens if they're so proud we can hear their shirt buttons popping right through the phone line?"

"Then you buy me dinner tomorrow."

"Hmm," she mused. "Either way we can't lose."

"That's how I see it. Now come on."

Matt practically dragged her back to her condo, then with trepidation, Tori dialed her parents' phone number.

"Hi, Mom."

"Victoria! I'm so glad you called. The whole family is here. You can talk to everyone."

"That's fine, Mom. But I have something to tell you first."

"You're getting married?"

"No. Listen . . . I—"

"Are you all right? Do you need money? Are you coming home?"

She looked at Matt and rolled her eyes. "No, I'm not coming home, and I'm fine. As far as money—"

"I knew it, Victoria. I knew you'd have trouble making a living."

"Motherrr! Listen for a minute."

"Don't take that tone with me, Victoria Denise Gordon."

"Sorry, Mom." Tori made a face. "Please, just listen to me."

"I have been listening. If you have something to say, why don't you just say it?"

Give me patience, Tori prayed. Before her mother could say anything else, she blurted, "Isoldaveryexpensivehouse andearnedaverybigcommission."

"What was that, honey? You know I can't understand you when you talk so fast."

Tori sighed. This was hopeless. If Matt hadn't been standing right beside her, she would probably have said goodbye and hung up.

Once again, this time very slowly, enunciating every word, Tori said, "I sold a very expensive house and earned a very big commission."

Matt didn't take his eyes off Victoria. The expression on her face kept changing from dismay to frustration and back again. Occasionally, she smiled. He couldn't decipher what any of it meant. At least she wasn't crying. He mentally crossed his fingers, hoping again that he hadn't given her bad advice. He wouldn't want to be responsible for causing her pain.

Her mother's response was exactly what Tori had anticipated. Without even bothering to ask how much money was involved, Mrs. Gordon said, "Does that mean you've got this career thing out of your system, and you're ready to come home?"

While Tori listened, first to her mother and father, then to her brother, she felt her heart shatter into tiny pieces. By now, her protective wall should have been solidly in place, but how could she insulate herself against being hurt by the people whose opinions meant so much?

Her father didn't even comment on her success. "I don't like that Alice Bensomething," he said. "How can you do business with a woman who has centerfold models on her show?"

At that, Tori gritted her teeth and fought back the tears. To hide her pain from Matt, she tried to grin, but she suspected it looked more like a grimace. She was ashamed to admit that her parents were so insensitive—especially since he, a stranger, had put so much faith in them.

Her brother came on the line, and his remarks stung like a swarm of killer bees. "That sale was a fluke. Take the money and come back home before you throw it all away. You'll never have another sale like it!"

Her hand was so damp, the phone almost slid out of her hand. Better if it did, she thought. Then she wouldn't have to listen to their putdowns anymore.

Finally her sister, Nan, took her turn. Tori held her breath, three down, only one more to go. She could handle it. She forced another smile for Matt's sake, then stared over his head at the Renoir print on the far wall.

"Way to go, Vic," Nan's sweet voice sang. "I knew you'd make something of yourself."

Tori caught her breath. Happiness flew through her like a flock of birds winging south. "Thanks, Nan."

"You always had that drive to succeed. I wish

150

I had the nerve to do what you did." Nan's voice drifted off as she spoke away from the phone. "Okay. I'm coming." Then she came back on the line. "I've gotta go. Write me a long letter and tell me how you're spending your money! You'd better be enjoying every penny of it. Heaven knows you've done without long enough."

Nan's enthusiasm pasted back some of the shards of her broken heart. Now she didn't have to lie to Matt. A member of her family really was pleased for her.

When Matt thought he couldn't contain his curiosity any longer, Victoria hung up.

"Well?" he asked, unable to read the answer from the bemused expression on her face.

She threw her arms around him. "I'm buying you the biggest, best dinner you've had since you moved to Florida!"

Chapter Eight

"That's not quite what I was looking for." Shaking her head, Tori pointed to the rack of clothing. "Let me see that blue dress."

Earlier that morning, she had returned to the Starlight Boutique on Worth Avenue where she'd made her first purchases after selling the house. For more than an hour the personal shopper had presented garment after garment for approval. Tori's head was swimming with colors and fabrics, styles and lengths.

The saleswoman turned her back as she reached for the dress, not hiding her annoyance very well. From all the clothing Tori had looked at and tried on, so far she'd chosen only two outfits—a pale green silk dress that she would wear that evening when she took Matt out for dinner and a lavender linen business suit.

"Madam." The saleswoman pushed her half-glasses further down her nose and looked over the tops at her customer. "Two weeks ago when you came in here and asked for guidance from a personal shopper, you made your needs quite clear. I can't imagine why nothing pleases you now. These garments are from our very finest collections."

"I'm sure they are." Tori tried to mimic the woman's snooty tone, but knew she couldn't possibly achieve that level of cultivated condescension. "However, most of these garments are offensively overpriced."

The saleswoman gasped. "But, madam—"

Tori stood up. "I'll just take these two."

The other woman started to say something, then apparently thought better of it. "Yes, madam." She stomped toward the customer service desk.

Mentally counting to ten, Tori strolled after her. The clothes she'd been shown had not only been overpriced, they weren't even stylish. This boutique, the same one where the clerk had encouraged her to buy the frumpy blue dress Wendy had ridiculed, was trying to take advantage of her by pushing outdated styles. Even angrier than the frustrated saleswoman, Tori snapped open her worn old purse and pulled out her checkbook. Having a lot of money didn't make her a fool. What a waste of time!

She wouldn't have bothered coming back to the store at all except that she'd left a deposit. But for that and the fact that the two garments she had chosen were perfect, she would have demanded her money back and walked out empty-handed. No point spiting herself.

Carrying the plastic-draped purchases by their hangers, she walked beneath Worth Avenue's arcades to her car. Matt should be pleased she'd bought only two items. But they were very expensive items — a fact which should add another frown line to the brow of her financial advisor. Especially since buying her new outfits had depleted her "play" fund.

She laid the clothes on the backseat and got in. The battered purse she tossed on the passenger seat looked as out of place on the shiny white leather as a pair of jeans at a fancy-dress ball. She had to buy herself a new one; she simply had to. If she didn't replace that handbag soon, it was going to fall apart while she carried it.

The minute she turned the ignition key, cool air gushed out of the air conditioner ducts. Grinning, she headed for the mall.

Luxuriating in the creature comforts of her new car, she thought about Matt. Actually, almost everything reminded her of him. When she wanted to spend money, he was her conscience warning her to be sensible. When she didn't spend it, her reward was knowing he'd be pleased. Men in cowboy hats reminded her of him. Or business suits. Or thigh-hugging jeans.

Just the memories of his kisses and caresses turned her insides to mush. No! She slammed her hand on the steering wheel. He wasn't for her. She needed someone who would draw her out of the shell she was pecking at like a hatching chick. Too serious, too cautious, he wouldn't help at all. Ah, but when she was with him, she forgot all that.

Oblivious to everything but Matt, Tori suddenly saw the mall on her right. She didn't even remember driving there. Somehow she had to prevent him from taking such a grip on her psyche.

She turned the car into the parking lot and found a spot near the entrance. Once in the department store, it didn't take long to find a reasonably priced, oversized leather handbag in a neutral bone color which coordinated with her wardrobe.

When she returned to the office after dropping the packages off at her condo, Irene handed her a message slip. "You had a call," the receptionist told her.

"Matt?" Tori asked hopefully, scanning the pink piece of paper. Not Matt. Her appointment for tomorrow had been cancelled and didn't reschedule. "Oh, no."

"He was a potential buyer, huh?"

"Yeah." Tori crumpled the paper and tossed it in the wastebasket. Her eyebrows lowered and she frowned. "I was really counting on that guy, too."

"There'll be others."

"There'd better be." The expensive life-style she was cultivating needed to be supported.

As she passed Wendy's desk, the blond realtor stopped her. "I'm showing that house in Boca this afternoon. Is there anything I should know about it?"

Tori shrugged. Why should she help Wendy? Because, her sensible self retorted, if she sells the house, they split the commission.

With a nod, Tori went to her desk, then came back with some photos and handed them over. "Look through these. They should give you a feel for the place. The owner's a really sweet old lady, and the house just oozes love."

Wendy waved her hand. "Yeah, right. I'll just tell that to my clients."

"Maybe you should. By the way, how did you like the concert?" Tori asked, opening her eyes wide.

Wendy grinned broadly and tipped her head to one side. "Oh, it was just . . . wonderful. I enjoyed every minute. Especially because I was sharing it with a very special man."

"What man was that?"

"Why Matt Claussen, of course. Didn't I tell you I was going with him?"

"I didn't know he was taking you. I must have misunderstood." Tori grinned. There was more pleasure in seeing Wendy squirm than coming right out and calling her a liar. "I thought you said he gave you the tickets."

The color drained from Wendy's usually rosy cheeks. "Is that what I said? Anyway, it was a wonderful concert."

"I'm sure it was." Tori nodded. "Good luck selling the house." All the way back to her desk, she hummed a happy song under her breath.

A short time later, Tori was concentrating on some paperwork when Dain startled her by tossing a stack of snapshots on her desk.

"Take a gander at these," he said.

She shuffled through them then looked up. "Boats?"

"Not just any old boat. My new cabin cruiser. How'd you like to go out on it this weekend?"

156

She sidestepped the invitation. "I didn't know you owned a boat."

"I just put a deposit on it. I'm taking it out for a trial run this weekend." He took the photos back. "Will you come with me?"

"Boating is a very expensive hobby. Don't you need every penny you have to invest in your new project?"

"You're beginning to sound like your friend Claussen. Don't worry your pretty little head about my finances. As soon as our real estate magazine gets going, I'll be worth millions. I'll afford it easily. Well, are you coming?"

"I don't know yet if I'll be free. I'm hoping to show some houses this weekend."

Shrugging, he started to move away then turned back. "By the way, did you buy any tickets for the Homeless Coalition's charity ball?"

"Not yet. I got the invitation in the mail but—"

"No buts, beautiful." He fiddled with a lock of her hair. "Since the Association of Realtors has adopted the coalition as its special charity, we should support the ball. Buy your block of tickets, and we'll invite some of our friends."

"What a wonderful idea!" Tori said, searching through her desk drawer until she found the order form. "I'll take care of it right now."

"Good. I'll do the invites. Let me know about Saturday. But don't wait too long." He walked directly to Wendy to show her the pictures. The implication was clear. Go with him or he'll take Wendy. Tori refused to be manipulated that way.

She definitely wouldn't go sailing with him, although the sport was one of the activities she'd put on her mental list of fun things to do. Besides, her work had to come first, and it was too early in the week to make weekend plans. Being fun-loving didn't mean putting aside her responsibilities. Didn't it?

Whoa! she said to herself. She was beginning to sound like Matt! Was she reverting to her old ways? A shudder ran through her. Never. Never again would she be frumpy. Never again would she settle for sitting in front of the TV with a bowl of popcorn when she could be dancing the night away, or going to rock concerts, or sailing, or doing any other of the fun things. She had enough money to buy and do anything she wanted.

Her phone buzzed.

"Tori Gordon."

"Hi. What time are you picking me up for dinner?"

Matt's voice washed over her like sunshine, and she forgot all about sailing. Dain might not have been in the room, for all the thought she gave him. "Hi, Matt," she said. "About seven."

"What time are our reservations?"

"Reservations?"

"Where are we going?"

Whoops, she thought. She'd forgotten all about choosing the restaurant and making the reservations. "It's a surprise."

"Uh-hum."

She switched the phone to her other ear. "But dress up."

"Of course. I know you're taking me someplace really special."

"Aren't you worth it?"

"You betcha."

"Give me your address and directions."

While he dictated, she wrote, impressed and at the same time surprised that he lived in a very fashionable section of town. Wasn't he the person who was always preaching about economy?

"Got it," she said, putting down the pen. "See you at seven."

"Would you like to come in for a drink and hors d'oeuvres first?" he asked.

"Yes, that sounds lovely." She'd like to see where he lived, how he lived. "Let's make it earlier then, shall we? About six-thirty. I'll make the, I mean, change the reservations to eight."

"See you then."

"Bye, Matt."

"Bye, Victoria."

"Tor—" But he'd already hung up.

Holding down the button, she realized she didn't have the vaguest idea where to take Matt. Her experiences in fine dining left much to be desired. Her glance fell on Dain. He would know. So would Wendy. But she'd go to McDonald's before she'd ask either of them.

She punched Irene's extension and keeping her voice very low, asked her recommendation. Irene suggested Chateau Francais, a French restaurant noted for its romantic ambience, its fine food, and extensive wine list. Even Tori had heard of it.

"Very, very expensive, though," Irene warned.

"It's the kind of place ordinary people go to only on special occasions."

"This is a special occasion. Besides, we're not ordinary." Although they were speaking on the phone, from where she was sitting, Tori could see Irene.

The receptionist's dark eyebrows shot up and her eyes widened. "Oh?" she asked. "Anything you want to share?"

Tori smiled broadly and winked. "I lost a bet."

"Now I understand." Irene nodded. "Who's the lucky guy? Not Dain, I hope." With a scowl, she looked at the realtor who was still showing his pictures to Wendy.

"Not Dain, no. But why don't you stop picking on him?"

"It's no secret that I don't like him," Irene said. "He's as superficial as laminate, and it's obvious he's after your money."

"Give me some credit. I know exactly where I stand with him."

"I hope you do, sweetie. Take my advice. If you enjoy his company, by all means go out with him. Use him like he hopes to use you. But don't give him any money, and don't let him . . . take advantage of you."

"He won't." Tori was trying very hard to hold on to her temper because she knew Irene meant well.

"So tell me who the lucky guy is tonight." The receptionist's bright smile was contagious. "Never mind. You don't have to tell me. It's Matt Claussen, isn't it?"

Tori smiled back. "Why do you think that?"

"Am I right?"

"You're right."

"Now he's one helluva guy. Hardworking. Smart. Successful. And gorgeous. If I wasn't an old married lady, I'd go after him myself."

"He's too hardworking, Irene. Too serious."

"And that's bad?"

"Yeah. For me, right now, it is. I need someone carefree, like Dain, to teach me how to let go of my inhibitions. Matt stifles me."

"I gotta get the other phone. Have fun tonight."

Tori called Chateau Francais to make reservations then pulled out the Yellow Pages and made another call. This was going to be the most special evening of her life. She would spare no expense. Hadn't she saved lots of money at the boutique by not buying very much? And even more at the mall because the purse she'd bought was practical and moderately priced? She could afford to treat Matt and herself to the best of everything. He would be so surprised, he'd be rattled out of his serious frame of mind.

She left work early to prepare for her date and after one quick stop, she went straight home.

There wasn't enough time to go to the beauty salon, so she washed and dried her hair herself. Her fingernails had already been done professionally, but she gave herself a pedicure because the shoes that matched the pale green dress were open-toed.

She took great care with her makeup and dabbed White Diamonds perfume on her pulse

161

points. She slipped her arms through the short sleeves of the new dress and studied her reflection with what she hoped was an objective eye. The V neck was deep, but not too revealing. A generous display of her trim leg peeked through the side slit when she took a step. She nodded her approval.

Still looking in the mirror, she ran a comb through her hair and clipped on faux diamond earrings. Should have bought the real thing, she told herself, while clasping a gold chain around her neck. The faux diamond drop which matched the earrings fell between her breasts like a lover's kiss.

Her image smiled back at her. What would it feel like if Matt's finger followed the lead of the fake jewel? His touch ignited her like a match. He would set her body on fire . . .

Finally, she picked up the special surprise she had for him and left her condo.

At exactly six-thirty, Tori was walking up the front path to Matt's house. The small yard was abloom with colorful flowers, from the deep purples of spicy-scented petunias to the happy yellows of snapdragons.

As if he'd been watching for her, Matt opened the door the moment she rang the bell. He wore a light gray suit, a white shirt, and a red print tie. His dark hair was combed back from his broad forehead. He made her heart thud as if she'd run up five flights of stairs. The scent of his aftershave went to her head like wine. Without thinking, she reached up on tiptoes and gave his smooth-shaven cheek a quick kiss.

As she stepped back, he looked her up and down, then grinned as if pleased with what he saw. "You look exceptionally lovely tonight, Victoria." Before she could respond, he put his hand on her waist and urged her inside. "Come on in."

In the small entryway, she handed him the little clear plastic box she'd been hiding behind her back.

"This is for you."

Laughing, he lifted the lid and took out a white rose boutonniere. "Thanks." His sparkling eyes met hers. "Put it on for me, will you?"

Taking the flower, she pulled out the pin inserted through the stem and carefully fastened the rose to the soft fabric of his lapel. Before dropping her hand, she let her fingers graze his smooth cheek.

He gripped her arms, holding her against him for a moment. "You're beautiful, Victoria. Lovelier than the rose."

He kissed her brow, then stepped back. "I have something for you, too."

"Oh?"

He took a rectangular velvet jeweler's box from his pocket and gave it to her.

She opened it and gasped. "A silver palm tree!" She removed the dainty piece from its box and held it in her palm, admiring it.

"A keepsake to remind you of our private beach party."

"Oh, Matt. It's so beautiful. As if I'd ever forget that day. We had so much fun." Standing on tiptoe, she lifted her face and kissed him on his cheek again.

The kiss of an angel, Matt thought. To his eyes, she seemed so radiant, an angel couldn't have been more lovely. "Want me to pin it on?"

When she nodded, he could see her joy in her eyes, in her happy smile, and his heart drummed against his ribs. He took the brooch and pinned it above her left breast, careful not to stick her, even more careful not to touch her. Because if he touched her, he wouldn't be able to stop.

"Come into the living room." He led the way toward the rear of the house. Through the French doors she could see that the house backed on one of Florida's many canals.

"Oh, how nice." She stood in front of the window. "Do you have a boat?" She thought of Dain's desire for a sailboat. How envious he'd be of Matt!

"No. Can't afford one yet. But I enjoy watching them."

Unlike Dain, Tori thought, who'd decided he could afford a boat just because the prospects were favorable. Which was better? she wondered. Which of the two men was getting more out of life? Dain who took what he could, when he could? Or Matt who waited patiently for the future?

Accepting the fluted glass he handed her, she said, "To the boat that'll one day be moored to that dock."

"To the Victoria G."

"You'd name it after me?"

"Don't you think it's a nice name?"

"Yes, but—"

"But nothing." He offered her a choice of tidbits on a serving plate. "Take one of these finger things."

She helped herself to a cracker with a piece of cheese on it. "Don't you ever want . . . things . . . now? Aren't you tired of waiting for someday?"

"No. I have what I need, and a lot of what I want. A comfortable house, a fancy car." He put down the plate.

"But you want the boat. I'll bet you can afford it."

"Maybe. There are things I want more. It's called being a responsible adult. I can understand that you wanted to buy new clothes and a nice car when you first earned all that money. You needed a new car, and I guess every woman has to have a new wardrobe." He shrugged. "But once you get the 'wants' out of your system, you should be able to put aside money for your future. Instead of having less of everything now, you'll afford all of everything later. And think of the fun you'll have anticipating."

"But what if it never happens, and you've put off the 'wants' for nothing?" she countered.

"It's a gamble. But that's life. If you have everything you want, what do you have to look forward to? There are things I want that I'll probably never have."

"Like the boat?"

"Oh, no." His gaze seemed to study the graceful sailboat drifting by. "I'll have the boat. But I have

165

to work hard now to get it. Do you understand?"

"Yes. Of course, I do."

He faced her. "What do you want, Victoria? What do you wish for?"

"I wished on a star once." She felt silly admitting that to him.

"And did you get your wish?"

"Yes."

"What was it?"

"I wished that someone would buy that Palm Beach mansion so that I would make the tremendous commission."

He smiled. "You sure did get your wish."

She didn't tell him about the other part of the wish—the part that would follow in the wake of her financial success. Some of it was already coming true. If not her whole family, at least her sister was accepting her desire for a career.

As for love—that would have to wait. She didn't want to love Matt. Loving him would complicate her life. She didn't want a man who worked too hard and saved his money for the future. She'd scrimped too long. For her the future had arrived.

"Victoria?"

Matt's use of her name made her aware that her thoughts were wandering. "Why won't you call me Tori?"

He touched her hair. "Because to me you'll always be Victoria."

"Oh, pooh." She grimaced. "Victoria was a frumpy square. She's gone forever."

"Victoria was a caring person, an honest businesswoman, a good human being. She was an intelligent lady with a good sense of humor. She was sensible. All right," he held up a hand and conceded, "maybe she did dress a bit . . . er . . . conservatively. But clothes are only on the outside and beauty is just skin-deep."

"Is that how you saw me?"

"Yes. I liked Victoria."

"Does that mean you don't like Tori?"

"I don't know her yet. I'm not sure that you do."

"Of course I know myself. And believe me, I like myself a lot better than that . . . that . . . nerd. Foolish woman. That's what I was."

"Don't put yourself down that way."

"I told you, that's not me. Not anymore."

"Too bad," he muttered.

"What?" she asked, not sure if she heard him right.

He shrugged. "Want to sit outside for a while? This is such a lovely time of day. And there's plenty of time before our reservation, isn't there?"

She nodded. He opened the door and she preceded him out to the screened Florida room. When she sat on a deck chair, he sat beside her.

Looking down at the palm tree pinned to her dress, she commented, "Isn't it funny that we both thought of giving something?"

"Not funny at all. We're on the same wavelength. I'll bet I even know where we're going tonight."

"If you lose," Tori cautioned, "you pay the check."

"In that case, I'll just wait and find out."

"Not a man to take risks, are you?"

"Depends on the stakes." He traced the curve of her cheek with his finger. "Now if you were the prize, I'd risk everything."

Did he meant that or was it just a bunch of pretty words? Batting her mascaraed eyelashes, she asked, "Everything? Matt Claussen, you surprise me."

"That's how I keep you on your toes."

His finger wandered downward from the center of her throat, paused at her collar bone, then kept on going, stopping just at the point of the V of her neckline. She closed her eyes as he drew a triangle on her skin, tracing the edges of the neckline and an imaginary stripe across the hollow of her throat where the false jewel nestled. A whirlpool of sensation followed his path and made her quiver. Far back in her mind, a bell jingled. A warning bell? Or those bells of love she'd heard about? Either way, she tried to switch off the sound and listened to the thump-thump of her heart.

When he stopped his arousing voyage on her skin, she opened her lids and met the darkest eyes she'd ever seen. Before she could speak or wonder at her responses, he kissed her. His lips were hard, his tongue demanding. As was hers. She wanted him, all of him, as she knew he wanted her.

His hand ventured inside her V neck, then lower, lower until it cupped her breast. She sighed against his lips and heard that ringing again.

She couldn't block it out. It rang and rang and rang. Finally, he pulled away.

"Damn," he said. "Who could that be?"

The doorbell was ringing. No wonder she couldn't turn off the chimes.

"Oh!" she exclaimed, straightening her dress. "It's time to go."

"Go! The hell with the reservation. I'll cook something here—later."

The bell rang again. "It's the driver." Tori stood up.

"What driver?" Matt asked, one eyebrow quirked as he patted down his hair. "What driver?" he repeated, following Tori as she headed for the door.

Chapter Nine

"We'll be right out," Tori said to the uniformed chauffeur who was waiting just outside Matt's house.

Standing behind her and looking over her shoulder, Matt said, "Victoria, you didn't."

With the door still ajar, she turned to him. "Of course I hired a limousine for the evening. Aren't you worth it?"

"It's so extravagant."

"Wouldn't you do it for me?"

"Depends on the occasion. Not for a dinner date. It's so . . . wasteful."

"Oh, Matt, you're impossible." She whirled around, and her skirt flared out, showing more than a glimpse of her thighs. "Don't you think a limousine is romantic?" she asked over her shoulder.

"I think an intimate dinner for two under the moon is romantic. I think a limousine is an oversized car."

She stomped out. Once again, he'd ruined her fun. The chauffeur held the door open for her and she slid in. All the way to the far side. Although Matt had complained about the limo, she noted that he had no qualms about climbing in beside her. Glaring at him, she had half a mind to dismiss the car and driver and let Matt do the driving.

"You ruined everything," she said, sulking against the door. "I planned an exciting, romantic evening. Now we might just as well go back to the Pink Shrimp."

When he edged closer, she tried to slide over even further, but she already was wedged as far as she could get.

"I always think of the Pink Shrimp as 'our' restaurant," he crooned. "What can be more romantic than returning to the place where it all started?" His index finger traced a fiery path along her bare arm.

She pulled away, annoyed that even when she was angry with him he could still light her fires.

The engine started, and the long automobile pulled away from the curb so smoothly, it was a moment before she realized they were moving. "The driver knows where we're going," she explained to Matt, who didn't seem to care. "That is if you still want to go now that you've ruined my plans. Or would you rather go to 'our' place?" Her words were cold and mocking.

Matt reached over and ran his finger up and down her arm again. "I still want to go wherever you chose. A bet is a bet." His voice sounded low and seductive. "I always collect my winnings." His fingers sneaked beneath her cap sleeve and caressed her shoulder.

If she had any sense, she'd push his hand away.

But whenever he touched her, the only senses still remaining were the ones he aroused.

"If you're sure," she said lamely.

"Oh, I'm sure."

The privacy glass behind the driver was in place, leaving them as good as alone. When he encircled her body with his arms and pulled her to him, the rose in his lapel, the flower she had given him, squashed between them. Its heady fragrance wreathed them in its scent. Her real world vanished, and they were the only two people in their own special place.

His lips touched hers, softly at first, then more demandingly. His tongue grazed her lower lip until she opened her mouth, inviting him in.

Just when she felt as if she were about to lose all control, he lifted his head, leaving her gasping for air.

"Still mad at me?" he asked in a voice so husky it was almost unrecognizable.

"Yes." Just because he kissed her until she was breathless didn't excuse him for being so insensitive to her feelings.

"Don't be. I've come to realize that being a passenger in a limousine is a very pleasant experience." His finger traced her neckline as he had done a little while ago in his house — with the same inflammatory results to her insides. "With that partition and the dark windows, it's the next best thing to being alone. If you had taken your car, we wouldn't have been able to . . . uh . . . do this." He claimed her lips again. "Or this," he said against her mouth and explored her tongue with his.

When Matt realized the car had stopped and the soft purr of the engine had ceased, he released her. Grinning, he watched her sit up straight and rearrange her clothing.

He glanced through the window and recognized the freestanding building that looked as if it had been moved stone by stone from the Spanish countryside. Bougainvillea tumbled from its red-tiled roof, and only a small, discreet sign in front of the carved oak door with its stained-glass windows gave evidence that it was a restaurant.

"Chateau Francais," Matt said. "I should have taken that bet."

"Have you been here before?"

He hesitated a moment. If he admitted the truth, she'd be disappointed. But he didn't want to lie to her, not ever.

"Yes."

She hung her head. "Oh."

He lifted her chin with his finger. "But not with the most beautiful realtor in all of Florida. Not with you." He traced the soft curve of her cheek. "You have excellent taste in restaurants. The food at Chateau Francais is great."

The car door opened then, and the driver stood at attention beside it, waiting for them to come out. As soon as Matt stood at the curb, he took Tori's hand to help her, then, when she was standing beside him, he tucked that hand into the crook of his arm.

Turning to the chauffeur, Tori said, "I'm not sure how long we'll be."

"Yes, ma'am," he said. "I'll be waiting right here for you and the gentleman."

Tori nodded her thanks, and she and Matt strolled into the restaurant where they were greeted by a tuxedoed maitre d'.

"*Bon soir, madame, m'sieur.* May I help you?"

He looked at Matt, but Tori said, "We have reservations. Gordon."

"*Oui, madame.* Your table is ready." His French accent was as thick as bouillabaisse. "Follow me, *s'il vous plait.*"

He led them through a maze of tables. Tori recognized a famous Hollywood couple, recently married. And one of Florida's senators was seated at a secluded corner table with a Palm Beach celebrity.

Jewels glittered on the necks, wrists, and fingers of the diners. Tori touched her silver palm tree and thought it was the nicest of all.

A strolling violinist serenaded, her music mellow and so romantic it brought a tear to Tori's eye.

Their table was set with ornate silverware, stemmed wineglasses, and a gilt service plate. Gracing the center of the ivory tablecloth was a crystal vase holding a spray of small pink and white orchids.

The maitre d' held the chair for Tori as she sat down, while Matt took the seat facing her. With a flourish, the man draped a linen napkin across her lap.

As soon as he marched away, Tori eagerly looked around. "Isn't this wonderful? So elegant."

Matt twisted in his chair to get a better view of the room and frowned. "You need to understand something about me," he said. "I come from a working class family. We weren't exactly poor, but we certainly weren't rich. My people didn't win lotteries or make killings in the stock market. Every penny was earned the hard way—through the sweat of our brows. Both my parents worked, and as soon as we were old enough, each of us kids got part-time jobs. We paid for the necessities first. If anything was left over, it went into the savings—for college and for that inevitable rainy day. If we wanted something extra, we worked extra for it. That philosophy is so ingrained, it's hard for me to change my way of thinking. And frankly, I'm not sure I want to."

"But—"

"No buts, Victoria. I realize I don't have to live austerely. Actually, by most standards, I'm living very well. I've earned a few bucks because I'm good at what I do."

"And successful at what you do."

"I am. But part of what you see is carefully culti-vated to give the right impression to my clients. The Cadillac, the office in the best part of Palm Beach, the good suits, are all part of the plan. Believe me, I'd be more comfortable driving an economical compact and wearing jeans. But I haven't been in business for myself all that long. It's way too soon to count my money and relax. I've worked too hard to get where I am to risk losing it."

He took her hand. "I'm trying to loosen up, to look at life differently, to see things as you do. I've come to the conclusion that our concepts of fun are very different."

Pad in hand, the waiter stopped beside their table and asked if they wanted cocktails. Tori shook her head. "I'd rather have wine." She looked at Matt, who indicated his agreement. "Would you choose it?"

"Sure." he studied the wine list and ordered a zinfandel.

"So what do *you* think is fun?" she asked him.

"Having dinner with a beautiful woman."

She smiled, her tears long since dried up and forgotten. "What else?"

"Necking in a limousine."

"Mmmm. Anything else?"

"Indoor picnics. Movies. Concerts. A good book. Water sports. A drive along the coast."

Tori asked, "Where have you gone?"

"As far north as Daytona Beach and south to Key West."

"I've never been to the Keys, much less Key West. Is it nice?"

"Sure is. Very quaint. There's the Conch Tour Train which takes visitors to points of interest like Ernest Hemingway's house. Plenty of beaches, of course. Snorkeling. Reef diving. You'd like it. You should go there sometime."

Just then the waiter came with the wine. He splashed a little into Matt's glass for him to taste. When Matt nodded his approval, the man poured wine into both their glasses and left them alone.

They clinked their goblets. "To fun," Tori toasted.

"To losing bets." Matt took a sip, then, hoping to convince her he was the fun guy she was looking for, said, "I have an idea."

"Oh?"

"A friend of mine has a vacation place on Islamorada in the Keys. He only goes there on weekends but lets me use it anytime I want during the week. Why don't we take off for a couple of days and go down there? Think you can get away?"

She smiled. "Sounds like fun. But—"

He knew exactly what her objection would be, and he cut her off before she could voice it. "It's a two-bedroom cottage. You can have your own room." Although once they were down there, he'd wine and dine her and create an atmosphere so romantic, she'd be more than happy to share his room and his bed. He felt a tightening in his groin just thinking about the possibilities.

"Sounds wonderful. When?"

He shrugged. "Sometime next week okay?"

She nodded.

"Good. As soon as I clear the date with my buddy, I'll let you know."

"Okay." Two days with Matt. Alone! Tori picked up her menu as a shield to hide her excitement. "Now that's settled, what would you like to eat?" Peeking over the top, she saw that his eyes were sparkling.

He asked, "Can I order anything I want?"

"Of course. Start with an appetizer. I'll have the . . . um . . . shrimp cocktail."

"Not escargots?"

"No. I tried them once and didn't like them at all. Would you like to share a Caesar salad?"

"Sure. And the escargots. For the main course, *canard à l'orange.*"

"I haven't had duck in ages." She put down her menu. "I'll have the same." When the waiter came, Matt gave their orders.

A few minutes later, their appetizers were set before them. Tori admitted that Matt's snails, swimming in a garlic-butter sauce smelled delicious, but she refused to taste one. She'd been a good sport about the sushi, but snails were, in her estimation, the culinary equivalent to fried grasshoppers.

Their plates were whisked away and immediately replaced by their salad and rolls.

"This is very good," she said eating the last of her lettuce drenched in the highly seasoned dressing. "You have to admit that it's nice to do something extravagant now and then." She broke off a piece of roll. "I certainly don't plan to eat here every night, but after years of fast food, this is heaven."

He nodded. "I have to agree with you there. Except for me it's been mostly microwaved meals."

"But when you went out . . .?"

"You must think my love life rivals Don Juan. I don't go out all that often."

"Yeah, right. A guy like you," she scoffed. "I'll bet the women just drop at your feet."

"You didn't."

"Huh?" Holding the piece of bread, Tori's hand stopped halfway to her mouth.

"I asked you out, maybe ten times, and you didn't give me a tumble."

She put the roll back on the plate. "You never." If a man like Matt had asked her out, the old Victoria would have fallen over in a faint from the shock.

"Just a couple of weeks ago I invited you to lunch."

"I don't remember." What she did remember was that she hadn't taken him seriously.

"Just because you had eyes only for The J — I mean Becker."

Tori noticed that when he mentioned Dain's name, a look of disgust crossed his face. For a moment she thought about defending her friend, then decided he had no place in this special evening with her and Matt.

The service was so efficient that the platters of duck appeared in front of them almost as if by magic. Matt poured sauce over his crispy fowl and speared a glazed carrot with his fork.

As if their conversation hadn't been interrupted, Tori wondered, "You really asked me out? Before I turned blond?"

"I'm insulted that you don't remember." He popped the carrot into his mouth.

He affected an air of nonchalance, but he wouldn't look directly at her, as if he were trying to hide his true feelings.

"You mentioned something about lunch, but you never really asked me."

"Unfortunately, you're right. I didn't come right out and ask. Just hinted. Sent out feelers. Since you never picked up on it, I figured you were turning me down." He dug into his duck, still not meeting her eyes.

"And I didn't realize I was being asked. You were too subtle." The plate might not have been in front of her for all the attention she paid it.

"And if I'd have been more direct?" At last he looked straight at her, waiting for her answer.

She shrugged. "I'm not sure. First I was dating Eddie. Then, when we broke up, I swore off all men for a while." Finally, she started eating.

"And now?"

"Well, now, here we are. You. Me. Chateau Francais. Is this a date?" It felt like a date—violin music, soft lights, good food, and the man who ignited her passions with his smoldering looks sitting across from her.

"No. It's the payoff of a bet. When we have a date," he patted his chest, "I pay."

She took a forkful of duck. "I see." It was tender and sweet in contrast to the tangy orange sauce. "You're very old-fashioned."

"Very."

After the busboy removed their empty plates, the waiter came by with the pastry tray. "Our house specialty is baked Alaska."

"Sounds good to me," Tori said looking at Matt for confirmation.

He nodded and gave the order.

While the busboy set coffee cups in front of them, the waiter brought the dessert, a tall meringue-iced confection. He poured liqueur over the cake, struck a match, and set it afire. When the flame died down, he cut the cake in half and served it.

Tori took a bite. The sweetness of the meringue lingered on her tongue. "This is probably my favorite dessert."

"Better than Key lime pie?" he asked. It wasn't what he said, it was how he said it. Soft and low, like a caress.

Her stomach fluttered. "You can't compare the two."

Her tongue flickered out and licked her lower lip.

His eyes seemed to be following her actions, then he touched the corner of her mouth with his index finger.

"Oh?" he queried.

"The pie . . . has special significance." Her thoughts were swimming. What exactly were they talking about? Pie and cake, when all she could concentrate on was his finger caressing her mouth. With determination, she forced words past her tight throat. "Kind of like the Pink Shrimp."

"It's 'our' dessert?"

"Yeah." Our restaurant. Our dessert. Our party. Too many things were taking on too much significance, defining whatever was between them as a relationship. She simply wasn't ready for that to happen.

After she gave the waiter her credit card to pay the check, they lingered over their coffee. Finally she said, "Well, Mr. Claussen, our chariot awaits."

He laughed. "Let's go then."

The limo was at the curb and the driver hopped out when they left the restaurant. As Tori headed toward the car, Matt took her arm and stopped her. "It's a beautiful night. Do you want to walk for a bit?"

She nodded and told the chauffeur they'd be back in a little while. Matt's fingers intertwined with hers as they strolled.

They scooted across the street, dodging oncoming traffic. Safe on the opposite curb, Tori, laughing, looked into Matt's handsome, grinning face. Realization rattled her to the marrow of her bones. The man beside her was the only one in the world

181

she truly wanted to be with. Then came the joy. Exhilarating while at the same time frightening, it wrapped itself around her heart like a velvet-lined vise.

After traversing a small parking lot, they stepped onto the Lake Trail, a blacktopped path for walking and biking that curved around Lake Worth. The moon reflected its shining face on the water. An occasional boat cut a rippling wake in the otherwise serene surface. Stars flickered between fluffy clouds and the lights of West Palm Beach across the lake sparkled their own brand of magic.

Tori sighed. "It's because of nights like this that I left Minnesota."

She inhaled the damp, briny air. Not far away were the trappings of civilization, traffic noises, streetlights, homes — people — but here was serenity and solitude. And Matt.

"Um-hum," he agreed. She leaned her cheek on his shoulder, and he kissed the top of her head.

The touch was barely a whisper, but she felt it right down to her toes. They stopped walking, and he wrapped his arms around her. She edged her hands under his jacket then finger-walked up his spine. Her heart thumped in triple time.

Matt bent his head and kissed the curve of her neck. His tongue flicked her skin, savoring her sweetness. A taste here, a nibble there. Beneath his lips he felt the steady, rapid throb of her pulse, and he was lost. He had to have her, this enchantress who, unaware of her powers, nevertheless drew him as no other woman ever did or would again.

When he finally claimed her lips, her mouth was

warm and welcoming. Her essence engulfed him, swamping him with need. Another minute snagged within the captivation of her eager responses would make him want to take her right there beneath the palm trees and the starry sky. For the first time in his life, he was thinking in terms of love, commitment, marriage. Stop! he warned himself.

Not yet. Victoria still had to work out her priorities before he'd trust his heart to her.

With a groan he dragged his mouth away. "Not here, Victoria. You're driving me crazy."

As her hands tugged his shirt from his waistband at his back, she smiled up at him coyly. "I don't have that kind of power."

"The hell you don't." He reached behind him and grasped her hands, holding them away from his body. "If you don't stop that, you'll be sorry."

"Why? What will you do?" she taunted flirtatiously.

"Throw you down on that grass." He nodded at the area he meant. "Make love to you while anyone who happens to pass by can see us."

She gasped. "You wouldn't."

"Don't tempt me." He ground his pelvis into her abdomen so that she could feel the strength of the truth. "When I'm around you . . . this is what happens."

"Then I guess we should stop being around each other."

"You're kidding, right?"

"Right." She took his hand, and they started to retrace their steps. "As a matter of fact, I bought a block of tickets for the Homeless Coalition's charity ball. Would you like a ticket? We could go together."

He turned toward her and dropped her hand. Even in the dark, she could see his eyes flashing. "What exactly do you mean by a block?" he asked evenly.

By the measured tone of his voice, Tori could tell he was holding a tight rein on his reactions. Her sixth sense warned that what she chose to interpret as excitement was probably something completely different.

Lifting one shoulder, she told him she'd purchased twenty tickets.

"Oh no, Victoria!" he exploded. "Those tickets cost a fortune!"

Startled by his outburst, she jumped. "It's a good cause."

He lowered his voice a few decibels. "That's true. And it's tax deductible," he conceded. "But you can't afford to buy that many."

"Why not? I had more than enough money to cover it in my checking account."

"Did you pay for your stocks yet?"

"Well, actually . . . payment's not due for another couple of days."

"If you'd done some simple arithmetic, you'd have realized you won't have enough money now to make that payment. You'll have to dig into your reserve fund to cover both checks. And we set up that reserve so that you'd have money to play with."

Tori wished she were in California where there was the possibility of an earthquake that would open the ground and swallow her. She'd miscalculated her money and allowed Dain to manipulate

184

her. But it had been for such a good cause, how could she have refused?

Now that she was thinking clearly, she realized this new wrinkle would have been avoided if she'd bought fewer tickets. And she'd made such a big deal about the 'play money' fund. Now most of it would be gone.

They came to the waiting vehicle, and she told the driver to take them to Matt's address.

Everything wonderful that had passed between them just a few minutes earlier might never have happened. The atmosphere during the ride home was as frosty as the North Pole. Tori sat on her side of the limousine. Matt sat on his. They didn't touch. They didn't speak.

When they reached his house, he opened the car door and started to get out, then turned around. "Thanks for dinner."

"You're welcome." By the interior light, she saw that his face had become a mask. The sparkle in his eyes had gone, leaving a blankness that chilled her heart. Bracing herself for another outburst, knowing she was setting herself up for rejection, she said anyway, "The ticket is still yours if you want it."

"No thanks." His voice was as flat as his expression. "I've got a backlog of work to take care of. I doubt if I'll be able to go. Good night."

When the limo pulled away from the curb, Tori's vision was blurred with unshed tears.

Chapter Ten

Tori was at her desk trying to write an ad for another house she'd listed. But she couldn't concentrate. Matt's face wavered in front of the paper like a holographic image. *Go away,* she told him. *Go away and stop messing with my life. Let me enjoy myself and my money.*

She didn't want to be reminded of his anger nor of her body's heated responses to his caresses. She touched the palm tree pin on her blouse. She shouldn't have worn it. Should have locked it away in a drawer where it wouldn't taunt her. Better yet, she should have tossed it in the trash the way Matt discarded her feelings.

Wendy blew into the office like a whirlwind and came straight to Tori's desk. For once Tori welcomed the realtor's intrusion.

"I have clients who're interested in the house in Boca." Wendy's gestures were quick and choppy, and her face was flushed. She didn't sit down.

"They've made an offer! And they only want a 30-day escrow." She slapped the printed formal offer in front of Tori. "Here it is."

Not giving in to the excitement that was threatening to overshadow her distress about Matt, she took a moment to scan the pages. "This sounds reasonable, but it's less than the house is listed for. Let me check with Mrs. Bergman."

As she reached for the phone, she looked pointedly at Wendy, the need for privacy implicit in her expression. But Wendy sat down and leaned forward.

"I'll let you know," Tori insisted.

Slowly, Wendy got to her feet and strolled to her desk. Tori could feel the other realtor's eyes on her as she punched the phone buttons. When Mrs. Bergman, the owner, answered, Tori read her the particulars of the offer.

"That's perfect!" Mrs. Bergman exclaimed. "Take it!"

"Don't you want to negotiate? We probably could get another couple of thousand dollars."

"No. Accept the offer. Thirty days! I'll start packing this minute."

"Okay. I'll bring the papers to you this afternoon."

Even before Tori replaced the receiver, Wendy jumped up and hurried back.

"She's accepted the offer." Tori came around her desk and extended her hand. Ignoring the gesture, Wendy grasped her in a tight hug instead.

Her face still flushed, Wendy stepped back. "This is the most money I've ever made on a sale." Grudgingly, some of the happiness seeping from her voice, she added, "I have to hand it to you."

"To me? You made the sale."

"Yeah, but you showed me how to do it."

Tori couldn't believe her ears. Compliments and embraces from the high and mighty Wendy Neff? She held her breath, waiting for the other shoe to drop.

"We make quite a team," Wendy added, patting Tori's shoulder. "Wait till Dain hears. He'll be green with envy."

Across the office, Dain pushed back his chair and jumped up. "Wait till I hear what?"

"I just sold Tori's listing in Boca," Wendy told him as he came up to her.

"That's nice. Congratulations."

There wasn't much enthusiasm in his tone, and he rocked on the balls of his feet as if he didn't know what to do next. Tori understood his problem. He hadn't sold or listed a house in more than a month. Probably he was depressed. Feeling sorry for him, she decided to do something special to cheer him up. And with this new sale, there'd be plenty more money to do it right.

She took his arm. "What we need is a party."

"To celebrate?" he asked grudgingly.

"Sure. Why not? A change of routine will change your luck." An idea flashed into her mind, and she blurted it out before thinking. "I'm going to charter a yacht—"

"What a wonderful idea," Wendy exclaimed.

"—and invite all our friends."

Dain seemed to catch the women's enthusiasm.

"An overnight cruise to the Bahamas!" He squeezed Tori's hand which still rested lightly on his arm. "While you two attend to business, I'll call around and find out what kind of boats are available."

Self-doubt niggled at Tori's conscience. Her original idea of a simple party had grown into an extravagant cruise. Was she doing the right thing? She pushed away the thought.

As Dain sauntered back to his desk, Wendy said, "That was nice of you to plan a party to cheer him up. I almost feel sorry for the guy. He's really had a string of rotten luck lately."

"He had as much opportunity as you did."

"Sure he did. But he'd rather go with easy money schemes like that stupid magazine of his than find buyers."

"Don't you think the magazine is a good idea?" Tori was surprised at Wendy's comment. She'd always thought Wendy and Dain were good friends.

"The magazine is a good idea, but that Ellis character is an incompetent flimflam man. He couldn't make an airplane out of the paper, much less get the magazine into print." Her eyes rounded. "You didn't give him any money did you?"

Tori admitted, "Just a little." It occurred to her that this might be another of Wendy's manipulations. An attempt to put a wedge between her and Dain.

Wendy said, "Well, if you're smart you won't put up any more."

"Matt won't let me."

"Smart man, Matt Claussen." Wendy flicked her head so that her hair swung like a palomino's tail.

"I'll have to give him a call, now that I've got some money to invest."

Now it was Tori's turn to be jealous. She didn't want Wendy spending time with Matt. He was hers. No! He wasn't. She'd made it clear that she didn't want him. But she'd be damned if she let Wendy get those painted fingernails into him.

"The magazine will be ready for the printer early next week," Ellis Clayborne said.

Although he was speaking to Tori, his eyes rarely met hers. Rather, he looked over her head and scanned the fancy-dressed people dancing on the parquet floor and clustered around the lavish buffet table.

Despite Ellis's lack of enthusiasm for his publication, Tori felt a thrill of excitement. For more than one reason, she was really looking forward to the venture getting off the ground. First, the magazine filled a need in the industry, and she believed her ads would reach a wider market. Second, but more important to her, its success would prove to Matt that she hadn't been foolish to invest.

Dain asked Ellis, "Then we're right on schedule?"

"Absolutely," the gray-haired man assured them, his roving gaze finally coming to a stop on the cleavage revealed by the V neck of Tori's mint green dress. "The last several thousand dollars of seed money should be in my hands tonight, tomorrow at the latest, and I'll have the money to pay the printer up front. That was one of his demands. He didn't want to take a chance billing a new organization."

"I don't blame him," Tori concurred, self-consciously crossing her arm over her chest, pretending to scratch her shoulder. Ellis gave her the creeps. She hoped his professional behavior was more refined than his dealings with women. "He sounds like a good businessman to me."

The band began playing a loud upbeat tune, and Dain grabbed her arm. "Come on, babe. Let's dance." He didn't wait for her acceptance, merely pulled her forward until they got to the dance floor where other couples were already gyrating in approximate time to the rhythm.

For a moment Tori stood still while panic squashed the air out of her lungs. It had been years since she danced like this. However, as she studied the others to see if she could copy their intricate steps, she realized no one was paying any attention to her. They were concentrating on their own performances, while checking to see who was watching them.

Dain began swiveling his hips in time to the music, and Tori tentatively shuffled her feet. Before long, she was waving her arms, twisting her knees and pivoting her feet. This was her idea of a wonderful time!

Pleased that this charity ball at the country club was such a huge success, Tori basked in the thought that she'd been one of the major contributors—despite Matt's disapproval. Her purchase of the large block of tickets, as Dain had suggested—even though she found out later that he hadn't bought any himself—had pushed the receipts way above the organizer's goal.

Dain grabbed her hand and whirled her around. Was that Matt standing over there by the terrace door? It couldn't be, she realized. As far as she knew, he didn't have a ticket. She was twirled again, and the man was lost from her sight. In that short space of time, her pleasure in the success of the ball had been diminished. Believing she saw Matt brought back the pain of their quarrel.

As Dain spun her yet again, a tall, fair Adonis slapped him on the back and thanked him for the invitation to the ball. Tori raised an eyebrow when Dain merely said, "You're welcome," and didn't tell Adonis that Tori had paid for his ticket.

She hadn't even met most of her so-called guests. Dain had taken care of inviting them but hadn't bothered with introductions. It rankled her that so far only one couple had sought her out to thank her. Disillusioned and disappointed, she bit back an angry remark. This was definitely the wrong time and place to start an argument. But Dain would definitely hear her complaints soon.

When the upbeat medley ended, Tori left the dance floor while Dain stayed to fox-trot with someone else. Overheated from the dancing, she looked for a way out of the long ballroom, brilliantly lit by four shimmering crystal chandeliers and golden sconces along the walls. The French doors seemed far away across the crowd. Careful not to bump into the hands that held cocktail glasses or canapes, she edged her way toward the exit. Although she watched for him, she didn't see the man who looked like Matt.

At last she opened a door and with a sigh of relief,

stepped out onto the flagstone terrace. For a moment she stood still, inhaling the clean scent of newly mown grass. Despite the heaviness of the hot, humid air, it carried the tang of salt and was infinitely more pleasant to breathe than the smoky, perfumed atmosphere she'd left behind.

As she walked toward the wrought iron railing, she noticed a couple in the shadows, embracing. Above the strains of music coming through the closed terrace doors, Tori could hear the murmurs, but not their words. To give them privacy, she faced away from them.

Crossing her arms atop the railing, she gazed out at the golf course where eerie shadows, created by the full moon and the trees, cavorted. The offshore breeze shifted, and now she caught a whiff of Matt's distinctive aftershave.

Was he there? Quickly she turned. Except for the couple in the corner, she was alone.

In the few days since she'd taken Matt to dinner, she hadn't seen him. They'd spoken only once on the phone, and that was simply to bring her up to date on her investments. He hadn't even mentioned their tentative plans to visit the Keys. By now, she figured, after their most recent argument he was no longer interested in taking her. Besides, why would she want to go with him?

Because, she answered her own question, his kisses made her toes curl. She missed him. Her body ached for him. She wanted to talk to him, just to hear his voice. Even quarreling with him was better than no contact at all.

The citrusy aroma still tickled her nostrils. Where was it coming from?

The man and woman in the corner had blended into a single shadow. Could he be Matt? A pain pierced her heart, and she clutched the railing. Of course, he wasn't Matt.

Certainly Matt wasn't the only man who wore that brand of aftershave. Besides, hadn't he told her he had to work tonight? And if he were here, so what? He was nothing to her. Nothing but her financial advisor, a man who disapproved of every check she signed, every penny she spent. All he thought about was the bottom line and how to avoid red ink. The only interest he'd share with the guests at this party was the color of their money.

Many of the attendees were celebrities one read about in the tabloids, the wealthy who bought and sold expensive houses. Old, young. Rich, richer. People who knew how to get the most out of life, not the type who worried about how they spent their not-so-hard-earned money. She'd even had a brief chat with Alice Benning, the talk show hostess and new owner of the Palmworth mansion.

"What are you doing out here?" Dain's voice startled her, and she jumped.

She turned to face him. "Just needed some air."

"It's so hot and muggy out here, you could slice it with a knife," Dain said. "Come back inside where it's cool." He tweaked her curls. "The humidity's making your hair kink."

She made a wry face, but after one more glance at the couple in the corner, she allowed him to lead her back inside while she tried to tame her springy hair with her fingers. The band was playing a slow tune, and Dain steered her to the dance floor.

He wrapped his arms around her and jerked her against him. Although she tried to push back, his muscles became thick strong cords binding her to him. She kept her own arms stiff at her sides.

"Loosen up, Tori," he urged. "You're embarrassing me."

"Then hold me right." She pushed harder to open up some space between their bodies, but in vain. Then to her surprise, he stepped away from her slightly, dropped his left arm and took her hand. Now she put her other hand on his shoulder. "That's better," she said.

"No it's not," he said. "But it'll have to do. So tell me about that house Wendy sold. Will you girls make a lot of money?"

Tori nodded. "Not as much as last time, of course, and we're splitting the commission since it was my listing and her sale, but we'll earn plenty. Why?"

"Just wondering. You're getting to be a rich woman. And if Wendy continues at this rate, she's going to be rich, too. You women are taking over everything." His voice was sharp with bitterness.

"You had just as much opportunity as we did. As I recall," she said hotly, "you scoffed when I listed the house."

"No I didn't. I just didn't want you to waste your time."

The fingers at Tori's side dug into her flesh, and she twisted her waist to get him to ease the pressure. Obviously he was angry, but so was she.

"As it turned out," she chided, "I wasn't wasting my time, was I? Maybe you should have taken some of your clients to see it. Then you might have sold it instead of Wendy."

His feet stopped moving. "Let's go sit down. I don't feel like dancing anymore."

"Fine with me."

Dain made a beeline for Ellis, while Tori spotted a pair of writers she'd been talking to earlier and headed their way. Dain stopped short before reaching his destination, and Tori couldn't help but see the glare on his handsome features. Curious to learn what had pushed his nose out of joint, she followed his gaze and felt a jolt right down to her pedicured toes.

Matt, with Wendy beside him, was standing with a group of people just in front of the long buffet table. He had to work, did he? Apparently all it took to lure him away from his ledgers was the right woman.

Tori sucked in a shaky breath while the green demon of jealousy perched on her shoulder and stabbed relentlessly at her heart. Pasting a smile on her lips, she turned her back on the couple and continued walking toward her original destination, the writers and their friends. They greeted her warmly and absorbed her into their group like a drop of rain in a pond.

Her new acquaintances were witty and amusing, and Tori had—almost—forgotten about Matt and Wendy when she saw him approaching. She tried to step behind one of the bigger men, but she knew it was useless. Not only had Matt seen her, but he was heading directly toward her.

"Hello, Victoria," he said.

"Hi, Matt," she replied with forced lightness. "Let me introduce you."

"Not necessary. We all know each other."

"Yeah. Claussen and I played golf together on this very course just a couple of weeks ago. When are we gonna have that rematch you promised me?"

"Just name the day." The conversation centered around golf, a sport which didn't interest Tori. Even the other women were animatedly rehashing their game of that afternoon. Bored, Tori took the opportunity and started to drift away.

Matt grasped her arm. He pressed it against his side, keeping her next to him. When she tried to pull away, he held on tighter.

"I think Victoria wants to dance," he said when there was a lull in the conversation. "Please excuse us. Alvin, call me, and we'll set up a time for that golf game." As soon as they were out of earshot, Tori said between clenched teeth, "Let me go." He was pulling her along, and she stumbled.

"See. If I had let go of your hand, you'd probably have fallen. Too much champagne?"

"No. You're walking too fast." She tugged on her hand. "Let me go."

He dropped her hand, but by this time, they had reached the dance floor. Matt took her in his arms before she could escape.

Following his lead, she moved stiffly. Her heart pounded, and she had trouble catching her breath. From the exertion of rushing to the dance floor, she told herself. But her body betrayed her mind by responding to his familiar touch with all the longing she'd fought against all week.

Wanting to lay her head on his shoulder and relax in his embrace, she tightened her muscles until her neck hurt. Her back was rigid, as if a steel bar were thrust down her spine.

She said the first innocuous thing that came into her mind. "I didn't know you played golf."

"There's a lot about me you don't know."

She looked up at him. "Like what?" She felt the tension begin to ease out of her muscles although she tried to stay stiff and unrelenting. But she couldn't fight against his soothing touch.

"That I love the way your hair tumbles over my hand when I hold you."

Why was he behaving as if they hadn't quarreled? Surely he hadn't forgotten his coldness toward her, an attitude that had her tossing and turning with regrets every night since then. Had he missed her as much as she'd missed him? A flicker of hope sparked her curiosity, and she decided to play his game to see if he was leading where she wanted to go.

She shook her head and bent it back, letting her hair flow over his hand. "You don't mind that it's all kinky?"

"What does sex have to do with it?" he asked, his eyes twinkling.

Her brow wrinkled in confusion, but when she understood what he meant, she swatted him on the arm playfully. "The word has more than one meaning."

"Oh. Are you referring to all these curls?" His hand bunched the hair at the back of her head.

She nodded, enjoying the sensation of his fingers grazing her scalp. Even as one set of muscles relaxed, the rest of her tightened with revived wanting.

"What else don't I know about you?" This was turning out be a very pleasant game indeed.

"Um, let's see. You already know that I think we're a perfect fit." His hand strayed down her back and rested on her hip.

Her body remembered how it felt when he'd splayed his hand around her waist. She closed her eyes as desire fluttered through her. She wanted to get even closer to him, to feel her breasts squeezed to his chest. Instead, she forced herself to step back and opened her eyes. Enough of the fun and games. Time to find out what he was really up to.

"Did you come here with Wendy tonight?" she asked, inflicting self-induced pain. There was more than one issue they needed to resolve. "Is she your date?"

"Does it matter?"

"It. . . . No," she shook her head. "Of course not. If you want to take Wendy out, it's your business not mine. Except you told me you had to work tonight."

He grumbled something under his breath, but said, "I juggled some appointments and was able to get away after all. That's why we were late."

"So you are here together!"

"Yes. it was a last-minute thing. She asked me this afternoon when she called to discuss business."

That damned house in Boca, Tori thought. If she hadn't listed it, Wendy wouldn't have sold it. If

Wendy didn't have that commission, she wouldn't have an excuse for calling Matt. Damned house!

The green demon on her shoulder started jabbing at her again. The pain was overwhelming.

"I suppose you're here with Becker," Matt asked. "Where is he?"

"Last time I saw him he was hitting on Wendy." There. Maybe he'd be as jealous as she was.

"Now that she has a bit of money, he can spread himself around."

"You're cruel." She whirled out of his arms and made for the terrace.

Matt bit his tongue. When was he going to learn to watch his words? Victoria was still as bristly as a thistle when he insulted The Jerk. Ah, but when he calmed her down, she could be as soft as thistledown. He jammed his hands into his pockets. Anticipating the pleasure of making up, he followed her.

When he walked through the French doors onto the flagged terrace, he saw that Victoria was standing at the railing. He'd seen her standing there earlier, bathed in moonlight as she was now, her blond hair drifting around her like a halo. He'd started to approach her then, but The Jerk had brushed by him and joined her. Knowing how angry she would have been if he'd intruded, he'd stepped back into the ballroom before she could see him.

Now, however, Becker was working overtime trying to charm Wendy. Wendy, he knew, had no delusions about the other man. Her eyes were wide open. If she wanted to flirt with Becker, he wasn't going to interfere. Especially if it cleared the way for him with Victoria.

Matt had closed no more than half the space between them when Victoria turned as if she'd sensed his presence. Her scowl should have warned him away, but Matt Claussen was far from being a coward.

"I'm not cruel, Victoria," he said, as if the conversation hadn't been interrupted. "Just realistic. And if you'd only open those beautiful brown eyes of yours, you'd see exactly what I see." He touched her shoulder, but she shrugged away.

Turning to look out at the course again, she said, "Give me some credit. I'm not the fool you seem to think I am."

"I don't think you're a fool, but I do wonder why you put up with him." Tentatively he touched the back of her hand with his finger. When she didn't react, he laid his hand over her soft, smooth skin.

She shrugged. "I 'put up with him' as you say, because I really don't care what he does. But he takes me to places I've only dreamed about, and through him I've met people I never even dreamed I'd have the opportunity to meet."

"That doesn't really impress you."

"How do you know?"

"Because I know the difference between what you really like and what you'd like to like. Victoria, you have to be yourself."

"I am. You seem to think that deep down, I'm still Victoria. But the truth is, Victoria was the fake. Deep down I was always Tori." Or maybe a bit of both, she conceded to herself. But she'd never admit it to Matt.

Matt quirked an eyebrow. "Then you're using Becker."

Her shoulders sagged. "I guess I am."

"That's not very nice. What's he getting in exchange? Becker may be a jerk, but he's no fool."

She pulled her hand away. "What he's getting is no business of yours."

He looked at her askance. He truly believed there was enough Victoria left in Tori to have sense not to go to bed with Becker. The pain in Matt's midsection was so severe he almost doubled over. He should have tried harder to get her to go out with him before she sold that white elephant.

If she hadn't earned all that money, she'd still be plain, sweet Victoria Gordon. Victoria had common sense and ethics. She wouldn't use anyone, not even someone like Becker. The money had turned her into someone he didn't like very much, yet the attraction was still there, burning him. Either he had to bring out her best or exorcise her. Maybe if he could prove once and for all that he was the kind of guy who could fulfill all her needs, he could bring her around.

He pulled her into his arms. The lips he pressed against hers were hard and unyielding. His tongue rasped against her teeth.

Tori's passion rose like a relentless, storm-driven tide. Its power frightened her. "Matt!" she said against his lips, pushing on his chest. "Don't. Not like that."

"Why not? Isn't this what Becker would do? Grab

202

what he wants. Don't you want a take-charge kind of guy? I saw the way he held you when you were dancing."

She stepped back, and he released her. "You're frightening me." This wasn't typical Matt Claussen behavior. "Didn't you also see that I pulled away from him?"

"No. I couldn't watch." Matt lifted her chin and looked into her eyes. "I couldn't bear to see you in his arms." Then, out of the blue, he added, "I'm sorry I overreacted about the tickets to the ball. I have to learn to remember it's your money."

Eyes wide with surprise, Tori studied his face. The stony coldness of the other day was long gone. So was the flat mask which hid who knew how deep an emotion. Instead, his eyes burned with sincerity. His voice rang with truth.

"And I'm sorry I did such a stupid thing."

His finger on her chin singed her skin, and his lips radiated their own brand of heat. They held danger, even the destruction of who she wanted to be, but for the moment she didn't care.

She stood tiptoe and met his mouth with breathless desire. The band played a sentimental song. The full moon beamed a joyful blessing upon them. And the warm breeze enveloped them in the scent of flowers. But it was the touch of his fingers on her bare skin, of his lips on hers, that reaffirmed her blossoming love for him.

Voices intruded into their magic world. Other people had come out on the terrace. Reluctantly, they stepped apart.

His hand still held her arm loosely while they

leaned against the railing. "I spoke—" he broke off and cleared his throat. "I spoke to my buddy who has that place in Islamorada. We can have it next week. Still want to go?"

Did she? Did she want to be alone with Matt under one roof all night? When he'd first suggested the trip, he'd promised separate bedrooms, but she knew if she went with him, somehow they'd end up in the same bed.

"Same rules still apply?" she asked.

He nodded slowly. "You'll have your own bedroom."

Still she hesitated. Did she really have a choice? Was their fate inevitable?

Sounding like a TV hawker, he proclaimed, "And as an added inducement, I'll throw in all meals and maid service. No cooking. No cleaning. A complete, fun-filled, relaxing vacation. Entertainment included.

"What entertainment?"

"It's my surprise. I have a plan . . ."

"Oh?" she challenged. "Think you can top the indoor beach party?"

"No doubt about it."

"Then you're on." She laughed. Tori Gordon couldn't turn down such a delightful prospect. Especially since she wanted to go to the Keys, wanted to spend a few days alone with Matt. And if he wandered into her bed, so be it. Wasn't that something else she wanted?

"Nobody could refuse such a sales pitch," she said. "You're on. When will we go?"

"My calendar for Tuesday and Wednesday is

pretty light. Can you get away then, too?"

She nodded. "Um-hum. I don't have any appointments until the end of the week, and I can tie up any loose ends on Monday."

"Great! We'll leave early Tuesday morning. Spend Tuesday and Wednesday nights in the cottage . . . in separate bedrooms . . . and come home sometime Thursday, depending on our schedules. Okay?"

"Perfect."

"There you are!"

Startled, Matt tightened his hold on Tori's arms, but she turned around, and he had no choice but to release her.

Wendy's high heels clicked on the terrace floor as she hurried to Matt's side, while Dain curved a possessive arm around Tori's waist.

"What are you two doing out here?" Dain asked petulantly. "All the action's inside." He looked at Tori's lips and added, "Or is it?"

"Come on, Matt," Wendy urged, pulling on his hand. "Let's dance."

For the rest of the evening, Tori put on her happiest face. She was enjoying herself, wasn't she? Even though Matt danced with Wendy, ate with Wendy, laughed with Wendy, and didn't even look her way. The harder the green demon tried to find a permanent foothold on her shoulder, the more resolutely she shrugged it away. Matt might be spending the evening with Wendy, but most of next week he would be with her.

Deliberately and determinedly, she turned her back on the other couple. She was having too good a time for them to bother her.

Long after her feet started to ache from the dancing and her cheeks hurt from smiling, when only a few couples still remained in the huge ballroom, she and Dain said their goodbyes to the other guests. They joined a small group at the front entrance to wait for the valets to bring their cars around. Dain's came first.

He kissed her, then said, "I'm sorry you insisted on driving yourself tonight. I would have liked to have spent more time with you. But it's still not too late to go back to my place for a nightcap."

"Thanks," she replied, gently disengaging herself from his embrace and fighting the urge to wipe her mouth. "It's late, and since I'm showing a house early tomorrow morning, I'd better get to bed."

He leered at her, his eyes resting on the V of her neckline. "That can be arranged."

"That's not what I mean, and you know it." She laughed, pretending she believed he was teasing, wishing she'd worn a dress that showed less cleavage. "Good night, Dain."

"The evening doesn't have to end."

"Yes it does. Good night," she repeated, stepping back.

Dain finally jumped into his car and drove away.

The valet brought her BMW to the curb just as she saw Matt coming toward her. Standing beside the open door to wait for him, she thanked the youth and tipped him.

Matt came up to her. He put his hand on her shoulder, and his lips flickered against hers for a moment. "I didn't want you to go to sleep with Becker's kiss still on your lips," he whispered.

"Dream of me, Victoria."

"I always do," she confessed, then got into the car. "Good night, Matt."

"Pleasant dreams." He pushed down the car lock and shut the door.

Standing there, watching the sports car as it zipped down the road, he asked silently, *When are you going to come to your senses?* Was he talking to Victoria or himself, he wondered.

When he felt Wendy take his arm, he wrenched his eyes away from the road to turn toward her.

"Sorry I took so long," she said. "Clayborne was hitting me up for some money, and he wouldn't let me out of his clutches."

"Hope you didn't give him any."

She shook her head. "Not a dime. Want to come back to my place for a while?"

"Sorry. I still have work to finish tonight. By the way, thanks for inviting me to this ball."

"Oh, don't thank me," she replied. "Thank Dain. He gave me two tickets and told me to bring a friend."

Chapter Eleven

Tuesday morning, Tori awakened at dawn to a mockingbird's refrain. Its joyful warble reflected her own happiness. She'd been too excited to sleep much that night, and when she heard the first twitters of the birds preparing for a new day, she jumped out of bed, more than ready for her own adventure.

She stepped into rayon shorts on which multi-colored fish swam against a watery green background. The same pattern, highlighted with glittering paints, was repeated on her short-sleeved T-shirt. Although her fingers trembled with nervous excitement, she managed to twist her hair into a French braid, which bounced pertly against her back.

By the time Matt picked her up at seven-thirty, she'd tossed a few last-minute items into the small suitcase she'd packed the night before and was ready and waiting. Although nerves had twisted her stomach until it felt as tightly braided as her hair, she presented him with a calm, smiling face when she opened the door.

At her offer of coffee, he shook his head and said, "We can stop along the way, but we should hit the road now. If we're lucky, we'll be ahead of the rush-hour traffic." He picked up her bag.

Looking around, he asked, "Anything else going?"

"Of course. You really didn't think I'd have only one suitcase?" Hefting her nylon sports bag, she said, "I've got my snorkeling gear in here. You did promise snorkeling."

He grinned. "Sure did. Anything else?"

"No. Just my purse."

"And a jacket. Just in case."

After a quick nod, she took a tomato red windbreaker out of the hall closet and draped it over her arm.

"And a sun hat."

Tori snapped her fingers. "Right." From the same closet, she removed a wide-brimmed straw hat with a headband the same bright color as the jacket and tilted it onto her head.

He preceded her out the door, and while she locked up, he loaded the car.

Sitting beside him in the Cadillac, buckling her seat belt, she noticed that her fingers were still trembling. Why was she so nervous? This was Matt, her friend, her financial advisor, the man she l—liked. She'd never been nervous with him before. Then again, she'd never been on her way to spending a few days—and nights—with him before.

The traffic on I-95 was heavy, as Matt had predicted. "We'll stop in Fort Lauderdale for breakfast," he said. "That should break up the trip."

"Sounds good to me." Maybe by then, some of the kinks would have untwisted from her stomach.

For a while Tori chatted about her latest listings and potential sales. She made a cheerful comment when he told her his father was recuperating well, listened while he talked about his business, and laughed when he repeated amusing stories about his nieces and nephews. Some of the tension dissipated, but she still felt as excited as a high school freshman going to her first dance.

When they reached Fort Lauderdale, the traffic was slow but moving. "Hungry? Want to stop?" he asked.

Tori nodded. "One of those croissant breakfast sandwiches would hit the spot."

"Okay."

At the next exit he pulled off the interstate and found a fast-food restaurant less than a block away. Anxious to continue their journey, they ate quickly, and within twenty minutes, they were back on I-95.

Tori switched on the radio and pushed buttons until she heard the familiar twangs of a country music station. Words of love found and love lost filled the car. Matt reached over and turned it off.

Surprised, she asked, "Don't you like country music?"

"Usually. But it's too sad for today. I only want to hear good things. Don't you?"

She bobbed her head up and down emphatically. "Only happy thoughts." Which reminded her. "Ellis was supposed to take his magazine to the printer today. Isn't that great?"

"Sounds great. But I'll believe it when I see it."

"Matt, you're such a pessimist."

"No I'm not," he said. "It's just Clayborne. I don't trust him. Nothing I can put my finger on. Just a gut feeling. But my instincts have never let me down. That's why, since you insisted on investing with him, I advised you not to put in a lot."

Taking his eyes off the road for a second, he glanced at her. "It's not the publication I'm having trouble with," Matt insisted. "Just the publisher."

Tori crossed her arms and pressed her lips together. The man had a blind spot where Dain and his friends were concerned. The only way he'd come around to her way of thinking was to see how successful the venture was. Somehow she'd have to find the patience to wait until that happened.

She felt a smile tug at the corners of her mouth, and for the first time that morning she relaxed. What fun she'd have telling Matt, "I told you so." When she received her share of the earnings from the publication, she'd buy Matt an expensive gift. That should really twist the red-ink pen in his frugal ledger of a heart.

Staring through the windshield, she saw that the sky was filled with puffy clouds backdropped by patches of the bluest blue. Typical for that time of year, they'd probably drive into and out of rain several times before they reached their destination, she thought, thankful for the air conditioning that warded off the heat and humidity.

"So how are my investments doing?" she asked.

"Fine," he replied. "This month's interest check won't be very big since you didn't buy in until the middle of the accounting period. The amount is prorated. But next month, expect a big one."

She rubbed her hands together. "Good. I'm still working on my wardrobe."

Matt glanced at her, sorry he couldn't see the expression in her eyes which were hidden behind dark sunglasses. "You look good to me."

He wasn't too concerned about her wardrobe, except maybe a sexy negligee or those lacy things women seemed to like to wear under their clothes. Actually, he wouldn't mind seeing her without any clothes at all. He looked forward to their swim, conjecturing whether she wore a bikini that left little to the imagination, or one of those sexy one-piece things that kicked his imagination into overdrive. He couldn't wait to find out.

"Thanks," she said.

He glanced at her again and saw her smile. Her expression lit up her face and warmed his soul.

At last, they drove through Miami, and a short time later, Matt said, "Since this is your first visit to the Keys, we'll cross the toll bridge and take the scenic route, even though it's longer."

"We have plenty of time." Two whole days, she thought. And two whole nights. Her heart leaped into her throat, then seemed to settle in her stomach.

Tall pines lined the sides of the road, then as they crossed the bridge, she recognized mangrove trees, their clumped roots looking like small islands.

Huge nests, like inverted giants' hats, capped tall power poles. "Bald eagles?" she asked with excitement, thinking she saw a white head peeking out.

Matt shook his head. "Ospreys."

When she spotted one of the large fish hawks riding the currents overhead, her heart soared with it.

"This is the start of Key Largo," Matt said as they left the bridge and turned right. "We're almost at Islamorada now."

Tori was immediately disappointed. She'd expected lush vegetation, unparalleled ocean views, and luxurious homes and hotels. Instead, the road was lined with stores, billboards and gas stations—like Anytown, USA.

"Is this it?"

"Part of it. Not very pretty, huh? Just a few minutes more, and you'll understand why people come here from all over the world."

As they continued driving on U.S. Highway 1, he explained, "Those green signs we keep passing are mile markers. Instead of using postal addresses, most of the places here are simply indi-

213

cated by their nearest mile marker. Zero is at Key West."

"That's certainly unique."

Shortly after they reached Islamorada, Matt made a right turn onto a private road which took them past several small villas. "This is it," he said, parking in front of the last cottage in the row, a dome-shaped structure just a few feet from the beach on the Gulf of Mexico side of the island.

The moment he opened the door, sultry air filled the car interior. Before he could come around to her side, she opened her own door and stepped out. After the air conditioning, the heat and humidity made her feel as if she were in a rain forest. But the delightful tangy breeze which blew off the gulf made the climate bearable.

She was anxious to explore the unusually shaped building where she would spend the next two nights with Matt. Yet the inviting expanse of sea also drew her attention. A gull squawked as if calling to her, so she followed its lead to the beach. Blue water met blue sky far off on the horizon as seabirds wheeled overhead and dove, breaking the surface.

"What a sight," she whispered when Matt came up behind her.

"Yes, it is."

"Last one in's a rotten egg." She turned around only to find herself caught up in his arms.

He drew her close, and his warm breath caressed her neck as he held her. She closed her eyes and laid her cheek on his chest, listening to the thump of his heart. Finally he dropped a kiss on the top of her head and moved away, leaving her feeling empty and incomplete.

"The water will have to wait a few more minutes," he said. "We'd better bring in the stuff from the car first."

Hand in hand they walked back to the Cadillac, where he slung her sports bag over his shoulder and picked up their small overnight cases.

"I'll come back for the rest," he said as she grabbed a couple of grocery bags and started toward the weathered wood-faced structure.

The minute Matt unlocked the front door and they stepped inside the house, she was struck by the musty, closed-up smell. While he adjusted the air conditioner, she gazed up at the ceiling, three stories above her head. She trailed her fingers along one of the unusual octagon walls, then walked through to the kitchen. Food and water bowls on the floor near the back door, so clean they could have passed the reflection test, gave no hint of what species of pet shared the cottage with its owners.

"Dog or cat?" she asked, nodding at the bowls.

"Dog. A big, furry mutt." Matt held his hand about three feet above the floor. "Nice temperament, but sheds like hell." He walked back into the hallway leading from the living room.

"I'll take the master bedroom up there." He pointed toward the second level. A white railing curved in front of a balcony, but from where she stood, she couldn't see very far onto the landing.

He opened a door. "This'll be your room. It's not as big as mine, but as you can see, it has a door while mine is an open loft. You'll have more privacy in here."

A queen-sized bed against one of the oddly shaped walls dominated the area. Tori noticed that Matt couldn't seem to take his eyes off that bed. Heat flooded her cheeks while goose bumps tickled her spine. She forced herself to ignore him and walked across the braided rug to open the metal storm shutter. She gazed out through the window at the gulf, shimmering like a star sapphire. "It wouldn't be hard to learn to live like this."

"Unfortunately, it's only a vacation home. My friend has to work to pay for this luxury."

She turned toward Matt. "It was generous of him to let us borrow it."

"He's a nice guy." He opened a closet. "They've left some clothes in the closets and drawers, but there's still plenty of space for your things. The bath in the hall is all yours."

"Thanks. I'm sure I'll be very comfortable."

The cottage had all the amenities and then some of a luxury hotel, but she wasn't at all sure she'd be able to relax with Matt sleeping practically above her head in the loft. So close. Too close.

With one last lingering glance at the big bed, Matt backed into the hallway.

"Ready for a swim?" he asked.

"You bet!"

By the time they put away the perishable groceries and she'd unpacked a few necessities, the sun was at its zenith, and she was more than ready to hit the beach. She pulled the top of her new red bikini out of her suitcase and held it against her breasts. She'd bought the suit on impulse and tossed it into her bag at the last minute. Should she wear it? Did she have the nerve? The bikini fit her Tori Gordon image, while the hot pink one-piece she'd planned to wear was more suitable for the old Victoria. With a determined nod, she dug the bottoms from her luggage and slipped on the suit.

She stepped into water shoes but decided not to hide her body beneath a cover-up. They were only a few feet from the beach, so he'd see her in her skimpy suit soon enough.

Matt took one look at Victoria in her red bikini, and his imagination kicked into overdrive just as he knew it would. The leg openings cut an elastic arc almost up to her hip bone. The softly rounded tops of her breasts above the deep neckline taunted him. Tempting, so damned tempting. He stifled a groan. Did she know what she was doing to him?

"I . . . uh. . . ." He plopped the cowboy hat on his head, turned and picked up his snorkeling gear. He doubted if he'd get through the day, and had no intention of even trying to get through the night, without her.

"What?" she asked, as if she truly didn't know how she was affecting him.

Without turning around, he rushed out the door, asking, "Can you manage your own stuff?"

"Sure." Suspecting what might be bothering him, she grabbed the sports bag and the pair of beach towels he'd abandoned on the couch. She hurried after him. "Hey! Wait up." Wasn't it bothering her too? That muscular chest with just a spattering of dark hairs practically calling out for her to rest her head. Those broad shoulders, strong enough to lean on. The flat stomach and narrow hips inviting her touch . . .

He was wearing light blue boxer-style swim trunks. Conservative, they suited his personality. Yet the moment he'd dropped that cowboy hat on his dark head, his whole appearance changed. He looked dashing and roguish and very, very sexy.

By the time she caught up with him, he'd already spread the blanket on the hot sand. "What's your hurry?" she asked.

"No hurry. I just wanted to . . . uh . . . to get the blanket out so that you wouldn't burn your feet."

"Oh. That's very thoughtful of you." She looked down at her crimson nylon water shoes and shrugged. Maybe he didn't realize she was wearing them.

She tossed the sports bag on the blanket and plunked down beside it. At her gentle tugging, the zipper slid open. One item at a time, she pulled out her snorkeling equipment.

"Are you ready?"

"Almost." Knowing from sad experience that her fair complexion would burn and blister in the tropical sunshine, she unscrewed the lid off a bottle of sunscreen and slathered it on her arms, then on her legs.

Matt watched the movements of her hands as if hypnotized. His palm could almost feel the glide on that silky skin. Now her hand was rubbing the stuff on her chest. He swallowed and turned away, making himself busy inspecting his snorkeling gear.

"Matt, would you rub this on my back, please?"

He groaned inwardly. "Isn't that stuff just going to wash off?"

"It's waterproof."

"Oh." Reluctant to touch her, knowing what it would do to him, yet aching to feel her body beneath his palms, he took the sunscreen from her.

Her skin felt just as he'd remembered. Soft and silky. Moist and slippery from the oil. Hot from the sun. His strokes were light and gentle, but he knew from the tightening he felt low in his stomach that if he didn't put a stop to this, he would have to drag her back to the cottage. He was just glad that he wasn't wearing one of those skimpy Speedos. He tossed the bottle into the open bag.

Pulling a plain white T-shirt over her head, Tori said, "I'm not taking any chances with that sun."

"I don't blame you." For a moment, he regretted that Victoria was covering herself up. Then he remembered T-shirts tended to cling — provocatively — when wet. "That sun can be pretty brutal."

She nodded. "I know." She picked up a swim fin. "Ready to go snorkeling?" Her toes slid into the foot opening easily enough but no matter how hard she tried, the strap wouldn't pull over her heel.

After she struggled for a minute or so, she realized Matt wasn't getting into his own gear. She looked up at him. He was standing beside the blanket, his hands on his hips, a smile that bordered on a smirk on his face.

"What?" She felt as if she were doing something wrong but didn't know what—like a guest using the wrong fork at a banquet.

"You have snorkeled before?" he asked.

"Well," she hedged. "Once."

"And?"

"And nothing. I snorkeled once." In a tiny voice she added, "When I was twelve."

"That's unbelievable," he exclaimed. "You've lived in Florida all these years, and you haven't snorkeled in how long?"

"Sixteen years. I told you I wasn't having much fun."

"You should have told me you couldn't snorkel."

"It's okay. I can," she insisted. "I remember how. I practiced in the pool." She perked up. "And I'm an excellent swimmer. Anything I forgot, you can show me."

He looked heavenward. "What makes you so sure I can snorkel?"

That took her by surprise. She gaped at him. Was he implying that he didn't know how to snorkel, either? It never occurred to her that he might

220

not. In her mind, Matt Claussen could do anything.

And that was another surprise. When had she started attributing superman qualities to him? He had worked his way into her psyche so slowly and subtly that her consciousness wasn't even aware of his being there. Since that day of their impromptu private beach party, she had begun to look at him differently. Sushi and inflatable palm trees had taught her that he wasn't the stodgy financial whiz whose feet were as strongly rooted to the ground as the mangrove was to the swamp. He was a man of so many dimensions, she had begun to expect more from him than he could probably produce.

"Can't you snorkel?" she asked at last.

"Of course I can."

"Really? Not just once when you were twelve?"

"Really. No self-respecting California surfer grows to adulthood without doing some snorkeling, or diving for that matter."

"You were a diver and surfer?"

"I *am* a surfer. Let's get you into those fins, and I'll show you how it all works."

"I really remember how," she insisted. "I just need help getting these flippers on."

"Hah," he scoffed. "That's because they're easier to put on if they're wet. Besides, it's hard to walk on the sand with them.

"Come on." He snagged his own snorkeling gear then offered her a hand up. "We'll make this a lot easier and do it at the water's edge."

Hand in hand they ran the few steps to the

shoreline over sand so hot it scorched their feet. Laughing she splashed into the water and sat down in the gently lapping surf.

As he knelt beside her and eased on the flippers, Tori noticed a small, angry welt above his ankle. "Looks like something bit you," she said, reaching over to touch the spot.

He scratched it, making it even redder. "Damned sand fleas," he said. "It'll go away."

She inspected her own tender skin. "They haven't been bothering me. You must taste very sweet."

"I'm giving away free samples. Want a taste?"

A flush colored her cheeks, but she touched his knee in a gesture that he took as a promise. "I avoid sweets before lunch," she said.

Before he could ask her when she did eat sweets, she tried to stand up, but the fins made her movements awkward. He put his hand on her arm to steady her.

Taking a step forward, she said, "Right now I'd like to go snorkeling." Without waiting to see if he was following, she waddled in.

Never taking his eyes off her, Matt quickly pulled on his own flippers. This was the first time he'd gotten a back view of Victoria in a bathing suit. He swallowed hard. The high leg openings of the suit revealed rounded half-moons, while the taut red fabric hugged the other half. Lord, he wished the water were cold.

After a short practice session close to shore, Tori felt comfortable enough with the breathing apparatus to venture further into the warm, clear water. She put her face down on the surface and started kicking, checking on Matt's position every couple of minutes.

As a school of mullet drifted by, she made a mental note to bring bread along next time. What fun it would be to feed the fish.

The water was so warm, she barely felt it on her skin. Sunlight filtered through the water, and she was glad she'd remembered the T-shirt. Sunburn would ruin the vacation as surely as poison ivy. Chasing the school of fish, she didn't realize how far she'd gone. When she raised her head to look around, she didn't see Matt. But the shore seemed very far away.

For a moment, she felt frightened. Then she caught hold of herself. As long as she didn't panic, she was safe. She could see the shore, so she wasn't lost. She was a strong swimmer, and there was no undertow. Here the Gulf was as calm as a lagoon. And, she realized, the water was shallow.

She lowered her feet and felt the firmness of the sandy bottom. When she stood straight, the water came up to her shoulders. Pushing her yellow swim mask above her brow, she saw, not far away at all, a snorkel sticking out like a periscope. Within moments, Matt was beside her. She'd been foolish to think he would lose sight of her.

He stood up, pushed back his own mask, and spat out the snorkel. "What's the matter?"

"Nothing. Just looking around. It's wonderful, isn't it?"

"Yeah. Have you had enough? We shouldn't overdo it the first day. Besides I'm hungry." Hungry for food, anyway. His hunger for Victoria gnawed at his insides. Tonight. That promise to himself kept him going through the day.

Victoria jackknifed into the water and began swimming toward shore. Through the clear water, he could see the graceful movement of her body. He remembered that he'd promised Victoria she'd have a private bedroom—and he'd kept his word. But he hadn't said anything about sharing the living room rug. His insides clenched just thinking about the evening ahead. He'd planned the scene of seduction down to the last detail. The champagne was chilling. The candles and compact disk were in his suitcase. He'd arranged to have flowers delivered and made dinner reservations at one of the best restaurants in the Keys. Everything was set.

With a grin, he stood up in the surf and waded ashore.

"What's so funny?" she asked while she ran a towel over her dripping brow.

"Funny? Nothing. Why?"

"Because you're smiling like the cat that caught the canary."

Almost, he thought. Almost. "I'm just happy to be here with you." He popped his cowboy hat on his head. "Come on. Let's go get some lunch."

After lunch at a local cafe, they returned to the cottage. While Matt put away the rest of the groceries, Tori went to her room to finish unpacking. She was hanging up a blouse when the doorbell rang.

"Victoria, would you get that, please. My hands are full."

Wondering who could be visiting them, she threw open the door. A delivery man, holding a long white florist's box, was standing on the stoop. "Miss . . . uh . . . ," he consulted his pad, "Gordon?"

"Yes."

"These are for you." He thrust the box into her arms.

She accepted the box while Matt, she noticed, tipped the man. Through the clear plastic lid, she could see roses. Beautiful, long-stemmed, red roses. She pulled open the lid and was immediately enveloped by their perfume. Taking them out, she cradled them, burying her nose in their fragrance. Then she looked up at Matt.

His blue eyes were sparkling, and that dimple in his cheek was winking at her. He looked so happy, so pleased with himself.

"Thank you, Matt. They're gorgeous." She reached up to hug him, careful not to crush the flowers between them.

"You're welcome. I hope you like them."

"I love them!"

He never stopped surprising her, she thought.

Always found new ways to delight her. He was still smiling, and she stretched on tiptoes to kiss his dimple.

"We'd better find a vase before the roses wilt," she said finally.

After she had arranged the roses in a vase they found in a kitchen cabinet, they went back outside and sprawled in a pair of lounge chairs under a shady tree. Tori hadn't intended to sleep, just to relax while her food digested. But she'd tossed and turned most of the previous night, been up early, and spent a lot of time swimming. No wonder she was tired. The hot air, tempered by the tangy salt breeze, was soporific. Bees droned in a hibiscus bush nearby and birds twittered in the trees, a lullaby duet.

Although aware of every sound, of every puff of breeze that cooled her cheeks, of the floral essences that tickled her nose, her eyes remained closed. She drifted as if carried by the tide. Her body was totally aware of Matt on the chair beside her although their arms barely touched. She heard his soft breathing. They were wrapped together in a magical shell that let in only the most pleasant of sensations but locked out the real world.

Being with Matt was fun, she thought. *I don't have to spend money to have a good time.* Her eyes fluttered open, and she saw the cottage. It must have cost plenty. Even a relaxing afternoon on the beach ultimately required money—money she now possessed.

She looked at Matt. His cowboy hat was pulled

low over his eyes, and by the steady rise and fall of his chest, she suspected he was sleeping. Resisting the desire to feel the hard planes of his stomach beneath her palm, she closed her eyes and immediately the tide of sleep pulled her under again.

Matt called her name. "Victoria," his voice crooned. "Victoria." Something tickled her cheek, and she brushed it away. "Victoria." Now it landed on her chest and walked on tiptoes along the inner edge of her bathing suit top. She swatted. It must have flown away because she couldn't feel it anymore. "Victoria. This isn't my idea of fun." That same whatever it was cruised down her arm. She mumbled and shook her elbow.

Suddenly, she felt a feathery touch on her lips. Something moist and warm. She opened her eyes. Matt. She lowered her lashes and opened her mouth to let his tongue enter. Awakening supplanted lethargy. A strong ache of yearning spiraled through her body.

His finger pushed beneath her bathing suit and fondled her hardened nipple. She caught her breath and wrapped her arms around his back, pulling him closer.

The sharp yip of a dog startled them, shattering their protective shell of privacy, reminding Matt they were not on a secluded island. He pulled back with a sigh. "I'd forgotten where we were." He stood up and tossed his hat on his chair. "Ready for another dip?" Taking her hand, he pulled her up. On legs that felt disconnected from her body, she followed him back to the water.

They paddled around for a while, chasing brightly colored fish, until Tori felt waterlogged and exhausted.

Treading water, she pushed up her mask. "I've had enough," she said when Matt came up beside her.

Back at the beach, she plopped onto the blanket, and it took all Matt's willpower not to drop on top of her. She lay there, her arms spread out, her breasts heaving with the effort to catch her breath. Her braid had come loose and her wet hair streamed above her like a golden sea fan. A few wisps plastered to her cheeks. Wet, her hair appeared darker, close to its original color. From the neck up, she looked like the old Victoria. No makeup. Darkish hair. Face a mixture of vulnerability and innocence, with just enough worldliness thrown in to keep a man off kilter.

He stooped down and leaned over her, pushing the hair back from her face. Just as he'd done when she'd been dozing under the tree, he gently blew on her cheek. She opened her eyes. They were filled with laughter. But her lips remained still and hinted at unfulfilled promises — promises that he intended to collect on soon.

"So that's what it was. I thought it was an insect. But it was just someone bugging me."

He hunkered back and put his hand on his chest. "You insult me. I was seducing you."

She sat up, her expression serious. "You're always so honest. Sometimes your truth is brutal, but at least I know exactly where I stand with you."

He couldn't look her in the eye. His words were true, but it was what he didn't say that made him squirm with guilt. Now he wondered if he could go through with this planned seduction. A woman saying "I trust you" was like being splashed with a bucket of cold water.

Then his eyes fell on the curve of her breasts as she leaned forward. He could see almost to her nipples. He'd be a fool to throw away this golden opportunity. Tonight he'd make her his.

Chapter Twelve

Matt had made dinner reservations at a popular restaurant which overlooked the ocean. Although it was the middle of the week in the middle of the summer, they had to wait about fifteen minutes for their table.

They waited outside, watching the last magenta fingers of sunset fade to purple while gulls and pelicans flew silhouetted against the darkening sky. Tori noticed a ficus tree that took up an area as big as the building it shaded. Aerial roots, some almost the thickness of the original trunk, extended down from its branches. Wide-stemmed epiphyllums, with lovely pinkish white flowers, twined around the branches.

Awed, Tori didn't know what impressed her more, the beautiful plant or the giant tree on which it lived. Finally she said, "I've seen epiphyllums growing in pots and at botanical gardens but never like that. Do you suppose it's wild?"

"I have no idea. But that's how they must grow in the rain forest."

"Yeah," she said. "What a sight that must be." She closed her eyes and saw herself and Matt, naked like Adam and Eve, wrapped in the fiery glow of the setting sun which filtered through thick foliage. Exotic birds sang to them as he plucked a sweet-smelling flower and threaded it behind her ear. Then they ran toward a warm natural pool fed by a glittering waterfall. He took her in his arms and . . .

With his hand on the small of her back, Matt steered her toward the building. "How about a drink while we're waiting?"

"Okay." Reluctantly, she blinked away the fantasy. "But no wine with dinner then. Otherwise I'll get sloshed."

Matt didn't argue. He wanted Tori in complete control of her senses — and responses — not even tipsy. Several hours remained before he'd uncork that bottle of champagne chilling at the cottage. A good meal should soak up any effects of their before-dinner cocktail. He had no problem forgoing the bottle of wine with dinner.

Later, replete from their meal of conch chowder and locally caught pompano, they strolled back to the cottage hand in hand.

"That was delicious," Tori said.

"Mmm," he agreed.

The shell path crunched beneath their feet, and Tori was grateful for her flat-heeled sandals. The sea-cooled breeze insinuated itself around her legs and tried to lift the hem of her short skirt. With her free hand, she held it down. Grinning, Matt hoped the wind would win. Victoria had beautiful legs.

When they reached the cottage, by unspoken mutual consent, they bypassed it and walked to the beach where tiny waves lapped against the shore. A sliver of a moon cast a meager glow on the calm sea, but myriad stars winked in a rare unclouded sky.

Wanting to feel the cooled sand squish beneath her toes, Tori kicked off her sandals. Before she could reach down, Matt picked them up and slipped them into the back pockets of his slacks. With each step she angled closer to the surf, until her feet were splashing in the tepid water. Still wearing his deck shoes, Matt kept to the relative dryness of the sand.

Remembering the itchy welt he'd developed from the fleabite, Tori wondered if Matt kept his shoes on as protection against the tiny insects, or if it was simply too much bother taking off shoes and socks and rolling up the cuffs of his slacks. Or was it just typical of Matt's unadventurous side?

When a gust of wind whipped her hair across her face and blew her skirt embarrassingly high, Tori held down the skirt with one hand, and with the other she struggled futilely to keep her hair out of her eyes.

"I'm blowing away," she said. "Let's go in."

"Oh, I don't know," Matt replied, tilting his head to ogle her legs. "I'm enjoying the view."

Abruptly, she turned and the skirt twisted

around her, giving him another glimpse of well curved thighs. Then again, he thought, his body heating in anticipation, if she was ready to go back to the cottage, who was he to argue?

At the door, she balanced against his arm while she brushed the sand from her feet. He felt the tremor that ran through her when she touched him. Did that mean she was looking forward to the rest of the evening as much as he was? Still barefoot she followed him into the house.

The moment he crossed the threshold, his senses were overwhelmed by the sweetness of roses. He took her sandals out of his pockets and dropped them on the tile floor while he watched her cross the room and bury her pert nose in the bouquet on a living room table. She'd been delighted with the flowers. Step One had worked out perfectly, he thought with satisfaction.

"Want anything?" she asked, heading toward the kitchen. "I'm thirsty. Think I'll have one of those diet sodas you brought."

As she passed him, he grasped her arm. "I'll get it for you. You sit right here." He patted a cushion on the sofa. "You're my guest."

He hurried into the kitchen and took two cans of soda from the refrigerator. At the same time, he checked that the champagne bottle behind the carton of pop cans was chilled enough and still hidden. He didn't want her to discover his plan before he was ready.

He poured the soda into two ice-filled tumblers and carried them into the living room.

"Here." He handed her one and set his on a table.

"Thanks." She took a long drink.

He felt her eyes watching him as he stuck a compact disk into the player and hit the start button. Immediately, the poignant sounds of violins filled the room.

Step Two. Mentally, he brushed his hands together as he sat beside her.

She leaned back and said, "Mmmm. That music is relaxing and soothing. I love it."

It was supposed to be romantic and arousing, he thought, disappointed but undaunted.

He looked at her bare feet, propped on the ottoman in front of the couch. So small, so dainty, and so sexy with their nails painted the same color as her fingernails.

"Put your feet on my lap, and I'll massage them."

With a pleased grin, she swung around and did as he suggested.

Back and forth across her instep his hands went. Kneading, finding her most sensitive spots. When he looked at her face, he saw that she had closed her eyes, and a contented smile played on her tempting lips.

"That feels so good," she purred. "You're the best foot masseur in all the world.'"

"Only foot?"

She laughed, and her movements sent her heels rocking across his thigh toward his groin. He grabbed her toes to keep them from grazing that part of his body that was beginning to throb with wanting.

His ministrations expanded to her ankles. Soon, when he began to knead the muscles in her calves, Tori felt as if her body were relaxing and sparking at the same time.

He nibbled on a toe.

Her eyes flashed open, and she jerked her foot away. "What are you doing?"

"Nibbling on your toe."

"I know that. I mean what are you doing?"

"Starting the seduction of Victoria Gordon."

"You're serious, aren't you?" Her mouth went dry, and her palms moistened.

"Yup."

He broke the eye contact and bent over to strip off his shoes and socks.

For a while they sat side by side while she struggled with her conflicting desires. Wasn't this what she'd anticipated? Of course. But she'd expected him to be more subtle, to win her over with his kisses.

From time to time, he rubbed his bare foot against hers, sending an ache of need up her inner thighs. Each time she edged away.

"You're not going to seduce me." The heat in her midsection told her differently.

"Okay."

He said nothing more, just sat there quietly, staring at their feet side by side, rocking his big toe up and down.

"You're not going to seduce me," she repeated

235

when even the violins from the disc player couldn't fill the heavy silence between them.

"You've already said that."

Again silence. Finally curiosity overcame her other emotions. Remembering his organizational skills as demonstrated by his well-planned indoor beach party, she put her finger to the side of her chin and asked, "What exactly did you plan?"

"Since I'm not going to seduce you, I guess you'll never know."

"Aren't you even going to try?"

"You want me to?"

"Sure." Tori couldn't believe she'd said that. But hadn't she expected something of the sort when she'd agreed to come here with him? She wasn't naive. She knew that when the very air between a man and a woman sizzled, passion was inevitable. Wasn't it time for her to be honest with herself?

"If that's what you want . . ." He dropped his feet to the floor and disappeared up the winding staircase to the loft on the second level.

She heard the rasp of a zipper and shivered in anticipation. Was he undressing? What was he up to? Matt was so full of surprises, she wondered how she ever thought of him as serious and stodgy.

Moments later she heard him on the steps. From where she sat, the first things she saw were his bare feet and then the bottom of his slacks. She was bemused. If he was still dressed, what was that zipper sound?

When he fully rounded the last curve of the

stairway, she saw that he was holding two candles in silvery sticks. He must have had them in his suitcase, and what she'd heard was the bag opening.

Fascinated, she watched him put the candles on a low table. Then, from the two easy chairs that matched the sofa, he removed two pillows and dropped them atop the rug in front of the hearth.

"Sit over there," he said, plumping another pillow and carefully laying it next to the other.

She perched on top of the pillow, feeling like a queen on a throne.

"Not on the pillow. In front of it. Then recline against it."

Without a word, she did as he asked and found herself almost lying down. She had her doubts about the wisdom of her actions, but hadn't she stopped being sensible Victoria? She tried to appear relaxed although her entire body was tense, awaiting Matt's next move.

She followed him with her eyes as first he lit the candles, then went to turn off the living room light. The fluorescent bulb in the kitchen was now the only other illumination.

"I'll be right back," he said.

Flipping onto her stomach, she watched him go into the other room. He opened the refrigerator and removed something before passing out of view behind a wall. What was he up to now? She smiled. She had enjoyed every minute of her day with Matt. A delightful shiver feathered up her spine. She had no doubt that she was going to enjoy every minute of her seduction.

She heard a loud pop. Smiling, she turned over on her back and cradled her head on her crossed hands.

Champagne.

Candlelight.

Two dozen red roses.

Soft music.

They all added up to atmosphere with a capital A. When Matt set out to do something, she had to admit, he did it right.

He switched off the kitchen lights, throwing the cottage into blackness except for the flickering candlelight.

Dropping onto the pillow next to hers, he handed her a fluted glass filled with clear, sparkling champagne.

"To seduction," he toasted.

"I don't know if I should drink to that."

"Go ahead. You won't be sorry."

"Oh, I think I'm sorry already." But she took a sip. She even enjoyed the way the bubbles tickled her nose and throat.

Matt's voice was thick when he said, "Want to change into something more comfortable yet?"

"No. I'm fine."

"It's getting warm in here again."

"Open the window."

"The wind will blow out the candles."

"And we wouldn't want that, would we?"

"Definitely not. Without the flame, we'd be in

pitch darkness. Soft candlelight is required for seduction."

"Is it the law?"

"No. Just tradition. But just as binding."

She took another sip of wine. Something warm
and fuzzy settled in her stomach. From the champagne or Matt? Probably a little of both.

He took her glass away, and set it beside his on
the floor.

He came back to her and with his mouth on
hers, lowered her to the pillows like a sheik with
his harem girl. When she wrapped her arms
around him, she felt the burning skin of his
back against her arms. When had he removed
his shirt? The man was slick, she thought.
Slick and sexy. And the way he was touching
her, he'd have no trouble succeeding with his seduction.

That was her last conscious thought as sensation became paramount. While violins sighed an
accompaniment to her own soft moans, Matt
marched a parade of damp kisses up the side of
her neck and across her cheek until he found her
mouth.

Against her lips, he crooned her name. "Victoria. I've wanted you for so long."

She had no words for him, but she answered
just the same. With the hotness of her kiss, with
the burning of her touch.

When he found her nipples and pressed his
palms against them, she arched her back. His
hand cupped her breast. Desire splintered her

body into millions of wanting, aching cells. Matt, she thought, and was lost. Matt.

The elastic of her waistband rasped on her legs as he pulled off her skirt without breaking their kiss. Then the hardness of his bare thigh brushed against her hip, and she realized he had removed his trousers. As she ran her finger along his leg, she felt him shudder. Her breath caught. Would she ever breathe again?

Her heart thudded against Matt's palms. It was his doing, he exulted. Her heart raced for him. He pressed his lips to her throat and felt her pulse throb. For him. Only for him. His hand slid across her flat belly then lower. Her hot dampness was proof of her need for him. A need neither of them could deny any longer.

When she gasped, he glanced at her face. Her head was back, supported by his arm. Her eyes were closed. And in the flickering light, he could see her lips. Swollen from his kisses. Tempting him to claim them again.

Matt's desire prodded Tori's hip. Mere inches and two thin slices of fabric separated them. Running her hands across his back, she felt bumps where only moments before there's been smooth, masculine skin. A shiver of anticipation coursed through her. She rubbed his leg with her foot and the bumps were there, too. Suddenly her mind registered alarm. Was it normal for a man to have goose flesh while making love? She didn't think so. Besides, these were larger. Something was wrong.

"Matt," she said, pulling her mouth and body away.

"Hum?" He held her tight. "What?"

"Matt, are you okay?"

"Okay? I'm on fire. Can't you tell how badly I want you?" His hand grazed her breast.

"No, Matt. There's something wrong. Your skin feels funny."

He nuzzled her ear.' 'I want you so badly, my skin itches."

"That's exactly what I mean! Matt, put on the light."

"No." He claimed her lips and locked her to him.

Wrenching away, she scurried out of his reach and stood up to switch on a lamp. Blinking against the harsh light after the soft darkness, she looked first at his legs and then, because he was lying on his side, at his back. From his nape right down to the elastic of his white Jockey shorts, and down the leg he was scratching, he was dotted by large pink welts.

She dropped down beside him and touched one of the swollen spots. "I think you have some kind of terrible disease. Or else you're allergic to me."

He turned around and sat up in the same quick motion, reaching for her. As she sidestepped him, Tori could see the bulge in his shorts, but her attention was immediately drawn to the three large pink spots on his stomach. He scratched at a particularly large bump on his chest.

"Damn. Damn. Damn!" Matt said, looking at his body with dismay.

"What is it? I've never seen anything like it before." Then she pursed her lips and nodded. "Except this morning on the beach. When you said you were bitten by a sand flea. Matt, you're being devoured by fleas!"

Now she, too, began to feel the prickles of tiny bites on her exposed skin. "This place is infested. We'd better get out of here!"

He jumped to his feet, mumbling, "Some friend that guy turned out to be. His mutt draws fleas like a picnic attracts ants. He promised to have the place fumigated before we came down."

"Well, either he forgot or else it didn't work. You know how fleas are. The problem now is what do we do about your welts?"

"As you've probably figured out by now," he said, running up the stairs with Tori in his wake, "I'm allergic to fleabites."

"You're not going to go into shock like with bee stings are you?"

"No. But I'm itching like crazy."

He rushed into the bathroom and began fumbling through the medicine chest. "Here it is," he exclaimed as if he'd just discovered gold. "Calamine. Be a pal and put it on me." He handed her the bottle of pink lotion.

"There isn't enough here to cover all your bites. I think we should pack up and get out of here first. Hopefully, the bugs haven't stowed away in our luggage. We should spend the night in a motel and head for home in the morning. Maybe a bath in baking soda will help you."

"Maybe." Matt pulled on his pants.

Despite the miserable itching, his greater discomfort was watching her walk around in her sheer, skimpy panties. The tail of her blouse came down to her hips, but she didn't seem to realize that only the lowest buttons were still in their holes. Every time she moved, her shirt gaped open, offering him an unparalleled view of her breasts, barely covered by her lacy bra. He saw no more than he had that afternoon on the beach, yet after they'd come so close to making love, her revealing dishabille was even more provocative. He had to get her dressed and out of there before he took her right there on the bathroom floor, fleas be damned.

He started throwing his clothes haphazardly into his suitcase. "Go pack," he said over his shoulder. "And get dressed."

Tori looked down at herself and gasped. Quickly, as she hurried away, she began fastening her blouse. When she got to her room, she realized the buttons were crooked, but she didn't care. She'd fix them in the car. Right now, she had to gather her stuff together and get Matt out of the cottage. She didn't really know what kind of reaction he would have, despite his assurances that he wouldn't go into shock. Maybe they should find an emergency room.

When she made that suggestion a few minutes later as they drove away, he scoffed. "It's annoying, damned annoying, considering my planned seduction, and our almost . . . well . . . but it's not dangerous or life-threatening. I'll try that bath you suggested, then you can coat me with the calamine."

They were driving north, and Matt, who had refused her offer to drive, pulled into the first motel parking lot that had a vacancy sign As he started to get out of the car, she called him back. He paused and looked at her through the open car door.

"I know I promised you separate rooms," she said in an attempt at levity, "but I'd rather not leave you alone tonight. If you don't mind, just get one room."

He smirked and winked. "Anything to make you happy."

While she waited, she ran her tongue along her lower lip. It was tender from his kisses, and her body still ached with unreleased passion. Once settled in the hotel, and the fleabites attended to, would they pick up where they'd left off? From the looks of him, she doubted if he'd want to do anything but scratch the whole night. Served him right for trying to seduce a sweet young thing like her.

Dain would never try anything so subtle. He'd push for what he wanted, and it would be up to her to fend him off. But Matt, the man she considered stodgy and practical, created an old-fashioned love scene, as romantic as any movie.

She laughed, happily anticipating his next attempt.

In the motel room, while he soaked in a tub filled with the baking soda she'd found in the cottage kitchen, she rummaged through their two suitcases, unpacking only what she thought they'd need for the night. A pair of Jockey shorts for him, a cotton knit nightie for her. When her hand closed on a full box of condoms in his case, she chuckled. Obviously, those fleas had thwarted big plans.

As she slipped the nightgown over her head, she regretted not buying that beautiful silk peignoir she'd seen at the mall. Although she'd more than half expected they'd make love on this vacation, she hadn't thought he'd see her in her nightclothes.

Anyway, she suspected that right now he didn't care what she was wearing. He was consumed by a misery of itching. And the more he scratched, the larger the welts grew. She hoped the soak in the baking soda followed by a liberal application of calamine would ease his discomfort.

"How does that bath feel?" she called through the closed bathroom door.

"Why don't you come in and find out for yourself?"

Perhaps he wasn't as miserable as she'd thought. "You know, Matt. I think your only problem is your overactive libido."

"You know, Victoria. I quite agree with you. So are you going to come in here?"

"No." She opened the door and tossed his shorts through the crack, taking a quick look at the tub. His long body was folded into the small tub like an origami swan. His bent knees were jutting out of the water. "I don't know how you're going to manage it, but you'd better get your legs into the bath for a while."

Like a breaching whale, he heaved himself out of the tub. Quickly she shut the door.

A few minutes later, when he came out of the bathroom wearing his Jockey shorts but still toweling his hair dry, he said, "I half expected to see a blanket hanging between the two beds like in an old movie."

"I think our relationship has passed beyond the need for something like that. Besides, I want to be able to check on you while you're sleeping. I'm really worried about your reaction to those bites."

"Check all you want. But you don't need to worry. These welts'll be gone by morning. This isn't the first time this has happened."

Shaking the bottle of calamine, she looked at him askance. "I hope it was the first time the fleas interrupted a seduction."

"Sure was." He dropped onto the bed and pillowed his head on his hands. "Are you going to shake that stuff till it foams, or are you going to put it on?"

As she tipped some of the contents onto a cotton ball, she hoped the lotion was cold. Not only would it serve him right for his fresh mouth, but it would cool his ardor.

He rolled over and presented her with his back. Not very gently, she dabbed each bite with the cotton. He didn't even flinch as she worked from his neck down his back. When she came to the waistband of his shorts, she lowered it without hesitation and covered his backside with bright pink spots. Nice firm backside, she thought. Like the rest of him. Not an ounce of fat where it didn't belong. Muscles and sinew covered by taut skin. She snapped the elastic back into place around his waist. Down his legs she went until the line of lotion in the bottle had dropped below the middle.

When she dabbed the bottom of his foot, he started to turn over. "Wait," she said. "Let the stuff dry first."

"Blow on it," he suggested.

"Blow it out your ear," she replied.

"Why are you being so testy? Don't you like being Victoria Nightingale? Or are you disappointed that my seduction was interrupted?"

"I think I'm going to chill this calamine lotion in the freezer."

But he'd hit on the truth. She *was* disappointed. She'd finally let her body overrule her mind only to end up frustrated and ministering to a very stimulating patient. With sympathy, she imagined how he must feel. Not only were his best-laid plans thwarted, but he was suffering the slings and arrows of a flea circus.

He groaned as if in terrible pain.

Taking pity on him, she moved to the foot of the bed and blew on the wet calamine on his sole.

He pulled back his leg and flipped onto his back. "You're no Victoria Nightingale, that's for sure. Where's your compassion? Where's the TLC?"

Laughing, she said, "Just couldn't resist."

She bent over him to dab the cotton ball onto his face where one large red spot disfigured his cheek. She was already off balance, so it took just a slight pressure from the arm he snaked around her waist to pull her across his chest. His kiss, so hot and demanding it rolled from her lips right down to her toes, reminded her where they'd left off in the cottage. She pulled away before he could take them any further. Right now it was more important to attend to his bites.

Levering herself away from him, she balanced her knees on the edge of the bed and touched the cotton ball to the spots on his chest and stomach. When she reached the line where his tan ended, her hand hovered above it, frozen.

"Go ahead," he said. "I itch there too."

"I know you do," she whispered. "But I . . . can't. You'd better do it yourself."

At his laugh, she felt her already heated cheeks burn.

"Ah, Victoria. It's almost as easy for me to get a rise out of you as it is for you to get a rise out of me."

He took the cotton ball, popped up the waistband and coated whatever spots he found. Before he eased the elastic back into place, she glimpsed the thickening of dark hair way below his belly button.

A flush heated her from her toes to the dark roots of her blond hair. Quickly, with her head averted so that he couldn't see her face, she put the lotion on his legs and the tops of his feet. "I can't believe this'll all be gone by morning." One last dab on his big toe, and she was finished.

"Trust me."

"I do, Matt. I trust you. I believe everything you say. I . . ."

"You what?"

"Nothing." Was she going to say that she loved him? She scurried over to the other bed.

"Are you really going to sleep way over there?" he asked.

"Yes. It's better that way."

"For whom?"

"For you. For both of us."

"Not for me."

She pulled the blanket over her chest. "You'll need to spread out."

"Yeah. And my scratching would disturb your sleep."

"You'd better not scratch. It'll only cause an infection."

"Okay, Ms. Nightingale. I'll try not to. Do you think I should wear gloves?"

"Matt!"

He turned over on his side, facing her. "Good night, Victoria. I'll see you in the morning."

The morning.

If the bites did fade by morning, he'd be feeling better. And if he felt better. . . . That coil of heat

249

twisted through her body. "I hope you feel better." She reached up and turned off the light. "Good night."

"Victoria?"

"Hum?"

"I'm sorry I ruined your good time."

"Don't be silly. I had a wonderful time today. I'm only sorry you got bitten."

"I'll make it up to you. I promise."

Almost as if it were phosphorescent; his promise quivered in the dark between them. A delicious sense of anticipation curled through her. Matt always kept his promises.

Chapter Thirteen

That pesky bug was tickling Tori's cheek again. Futilely, she brushed at it. It wouldn't go away. Instead, it tiptoed along her face to her throat and down to her breast.

She tried to pull the blanket over her head. Although she yanked the satiny edge, it wouldn't move an inch. Sleep gave way to consciousness, and she forced open one eye.

Matt's face blurred into her line of vision. His lips were pursed, and she realized he was blowing his hot breath on her skin. Her other eye popped open. No wonder she couldn't move the blanket. His full length was sprawled over it, anchoring it beneath his body.

"What are you doing?"

"Waking you up."

"Why? What time is it?"

"Dunno."

Another puff of breath on the upper curve of

her breast sent a delicious shiver from her hairline right down to the ball of her foot.

"The sun is shining, though, so I guess I survived my terrible ordeal."

"How do you feel?" she asked.

"I have an itch more terrible than the ones I had last night."

She scooted up so that she was half sitting, then realized her mistake. While she'd slept, her nightie had twisted around her, pulling taut across one breast, baring the other. Matt's eyes gleamed as if there was a fire raging behind them. With a tug, she pulled the neck of her nightshirt up to a more modest level.

He reached up, obviously intending to return it to its original, more revealing level. She twisted out of his reach, knowing it was merely a delaying tactic. Before long, she'd be naked, locked in his embrace. She felt the hot flush which crept up her body.

Hoarsely, she said, "Let me see your bites."

"Okay." He nibbled on her throat.

She pushed him away. "That's not what I mean."

He rolled away and sprawled on his back, spreading his left arm so that it landed across her breasts.

"You're terrible this morning." She picked up his arm and dropped it at his side.

"Give me a chance. I'll show you how terrible I can be."

Grimacing, she scrutinized his chest and belly.

Faint pink splotches remained where the calamine had been applied, but the welts had almost disappeared. The same for his legs.

"Turn over. Let me check your back." The minute she told him to turn over, she saw the glint in his eyes and knew he was up to something.

Sure enough, he crisscrossed himself on her lap, wrapping his arm around her waist. Ignoring the persistent wave of desire that settled in her belly, she inspected the areas of his body he presented to her. Other than a pair of angry-looking welts on his shoulder, the only evidence of the problem he'd had was the polka dots of calamine.

She laughed. "You look like a leopard with pink spots."

"A leopard, huh? I can think of worse things."

With a gentle push on her ribs, he tumbled her over so that once again she was lying flat on the bed. He twisted around and pulled her to him.

"Victoria, I want you. Now," he said into her ear. "I've never in my life wanted anyone so much. Last night left me in agony."

She knew he wasn't talking about the fleabites, since she'd been up most of the night, checking that he was breathing properly, that he hadn't gone into anaphylactic shock. Only occasional scratching seemed to disturb his sleep. Apparently the calamine had done its job.

And then, reassured, she'd been so aware of him in the next bed that her own exquisite, aching need for him had kept her awake.

If deep, deep down she really was an uninhibited as she supposedly wanted to be, she would have crawled in beside him. Last night had taught her something about herself. She had a long way to go before really and truly becoming Tori—if that was what she wanted.

She curved her arms around his neck. "I tossed and turned most of the night, too."

No more words were necessary. With her actions, she showed him just how strongly she desired him. With her hot, dewy kisses, dabbed on each pink spot. With her touch, first feathery soft, then kneading, grinding, demanding.

Matt returned her kisses. Initiated others. His tongue teased the shell of her ear; his teeth nibbled on the lobe. Tori closed her eyes and let sensation flow over her—the heat of passion, the joy of love.

Love echoed through her mind and spread like sound waves through her body—to her heart, to her soul, to her deepest self. Now love drove her, making his touch even more arousing.

Her responses were primal. Instinctive. She had found her one and only mate. Her passion rose to match his. It raged as all-consuming as a forest fire, yet not destructive. Rather, she felt reborn. Even as her body was about to flare into a million sparks, for the first time in her life, she felt whole, complete. In her happiness, she pressed even closer to him, feeling every inch of his hard body against hers, driven by a need so great it couldn't be contained.

Matt knew he was beyond control. "You're so

beautiful," he murmured, unsure if he really spoke the words or just felt them in his heart.

She was beautiful. His own Venus. He was lost in her. In her sweet feminine fragrance. In her skin, soft and smooth as silk. And the way she tasted. Ambrosia. Honey.

Her curves fit his hands as if they'd been designed for him. As he caressed her breasts, her belly and lower, he watched her expression and saw ecstasy on the curve of her mouth, in her eyes, glazed with passion. His tongue traced her lips, and his blood pulsed through his veins down to the very center of his desire.

Now that he was holding her so closely, touching her so intimately, while her moans and rhythmic movements matched his, he knew what he'd known all along. She belonged in his arms, in his life. He wanted her beside him always, as his lover, as his mate. As his wife.

Love was the force that propelled the heat in his blood and made his heart tumble and twist. Sexual desire pushed him, but love inspired him.

Victoria was his!

When he nuzzled her throat, she moaned. The vibration caressed his lips and radiated to every aching part of him. He'd waited so long for her, and he wanted to savor every rapturous moment, but he couldn't hold back much longer. He needed her so badly.

"Now, Matt. I want you, Matt. Now." Her words were a plea which reached from her heart to his. From her throbbing body to his.

He was ready, more than ready and when he entered her, she was moist and tight and welcoming as a light in the window after a long trip. Now they traveled together, further and further, higher and higher. The destination was close. Closer. And then they reached it together. A voyage they'd never forget. A voyage that would be worth taking over and over.

Tori, wrapped in the comfort and security of Matt's arms, fell into a deep, contented sleep. Later, whether minutes or hours she didn't know, Matt awakened her with a trail of moist kisses that started at the tip of her nose and ended on the sole of her foot. Her body passed from the darkness of sleep to the light of total awareness in an instant. Without opening her eyes, she smiled and reached for him.

The first time, their lovemaking had begun at a highly aroused level and ended at a fevered, frenzied pitch. This time they started more slowly, tasting, exploring, learning. Like a flower bud, their passion opened slowly, a petal at a time, one response building on another, until it burst open in love and beauty.

"Thank you, Victoria," Matt whispered.

"For what?"

"For being you. For being my beautiful Venus."

His words filled her heart to overflowing. She ran her hands along his arms, then splayed her fingers on his back, and nestled her head on his chest. She wanted to answer him, to tell him that he was her Adonis, but her throat was so tight, she couldn't speak. Instead, she listened to the quick pumping of his heart and fell asleep to its hypnotic, assuring beat.

The next time she opened her eyes, she saw him, naked, rummaging through his suitcase. His back was toward her, and her eyes were drawn to his backside with its faint spackling of pink. To her disappointment, he pulled on a pair of white Jockey shorts, cutting off the attractive, tantalizing view.

"Matt?"

He turned. "You're awake."

"Um-hum." She boosted herself up on one elbow. "What're you doing?"

"I thought I'd try to find us some breakfast to bring back. I'm hungry, aren't you?"

"Actually, I'm pretty satisfied, but I don't think it would take much to stimulate my appetite."

He pulled on his jeans and winked. "Breakfast in bed — then dessert. Sound good?"

"Sounds wonderful."

"I'll be back soon. Is there anything special you want?"

"Just you," she said.

He crossed to the bed and kissed her. When at last he lifted his head, he said, "Hold that thought. I'll be back in a few minutes."

Reluctantly, she let him go. She didn't want breakfast. She wanted him. But then her stomach growled, telling her it had needs of its own.

As soon as the door of their room swung shut behind him, she hopped out of bed and headed for the shower. The tepid water washed away the last of the sleep cobwebs. As soapy froth bubbled around her feet, she knew that no amount of washing would ever remove the imprint he'd made on her body. She belonged to Matt, and he belonged to her. They belonged together.

How wrong she'd been to believe his practical nature was too serious for her fun-loving spirit. They complemented—completed—each other. She drew him out of his serious, responsible shell, while he kept her from flying off into never-never land.

Stepping out of the shower stall, she grabbed the towel and clutched it as it occurred to her that no words of love had been exchanged. She had no doubts about the depth of her love for him, but how did he feel about her? In a million thoughtful ways, he showed her he cared. By his steadfast pursuit. By his planned seduction. By the way he tried to loosen up and amuse her. Even the palm tree pin showed that he had a creative, generous streak. None of that proved he loved her. But, she smiled and began toweling her arms, all the evidence pointed in that direction.

When Matt returned, his eyes were drawn to Victoria, sitting up in the bed, her back propped against the cushioned headboard. She'd pulled the blue blanket above her breasts and tucked it beneath her arms. The interesting way the cover fell into peaks and valleys hinted that the rest of her was as bare as her arms and shoulders. He felt his body swell with the prospect of finding out for sure. Sunlight beamed through a chink in the curtain and settled on her hair, making it look like a golden halo. His angel, he thought. His love.

In a roundabout way, his seduction had worked. Even now, Victoria was in bed, waiting for him. If it wasn't that he needed food to give him the strength to make endless love to her, he'd forget about eating. But after breakfast, he'd stake his claims to her again, make her want him so badly that she'd never give him up. Whistling softly to himself, he began pulling fast-food croissants out of the bag.

They spent what was left of their vacation either frolicking in the sea or frolicking in bed. Tori, thriving on Matt's lovemaking, wondered why she had put him off as long as she had. Fun was a relative concept, she now understood. These few days were the most wonderful of her life.

Thursday afternoon, in her opinion, arrived way too soon. Reluctantly, they packed up the car and headed for home.

On the way, Tori said, "I was thinking . . ."

"Yes?"

"On Monday I had an offer for one of the Palm Beach houses I listed, and Wendy and I split a very nice commission on that property in Boca."

"That's great!" Matt patted her knee in a proprietary way that made her heart flutter. "Wendy already consulted me about investing her share. I thought we'd buy you some municipal bonds. Diversify some more."

"That's fine, but—"

"I don't think I'm going to like what comes after that but."

"Oh, I think you will. It's going to be great." She rubbed her hands together gleefully.

"What is?" His voice sounded cautious, and she noticed the deep, troubled furrow between his brows.

Ignoring the warning signals, she plunged on. "I've been checking with travel agents, and I've decided to charter a yacht for a weekend cruise, probably to the Bahamas. Dain and I discussed it the other day. He thinks it's a great idea. I'll invite all my new friends. We'll have the greatest time. Those people really know how to party."

To her surprise, Matt pulled the car over to the side of the road.

Before she could question his action, he said, "I don't believe you."

His brows were lowered, and his anger flashed in his eyes.

"I don't know why you're angry," she said.

"You don't? Then you don't know me at all. Then these past two days together were a farce." A muscle jumped in his jaw, and she could tell that he was clenching his teeth.

"Our vacation wasn't a farce. It was wonderful." She ached to touch his arm but didn't. "I hoped that we would be together on the yacht. Share a cabin. You didn't think I'd exclude you, did you? Don't you want to be with me any more?"

She saw his chest expand with a deep breath, and slowly the tenseness in his muscles seemed to relax. The anger left his eyes. But the chill that replaced it could have frozen all the water in the Gulf of Mexico.

She wished he would talk to her and tell her what she'd said or done to cause this reaction. It had to be the money thing again, she thought. Right from the start, she'd felt that a relationship between them would be doomed. Their ways of looking at money and how to spend it were too different. Because his kisses turned her body inside out, she'd tossed those concerns aside. What a fool she'd been.

"No, Tori," he said in a calm, even tone. "I didn't doubt that you'd invite me. It's those shallow users you call friends that I thought you were finished with — and Becker."

"So that's it. You're jealous."

"Maybe I am," he said, clenching his teeth again. "But I'll tell you this. You looked a lot better to me when you were plain and poor." Without another glance at her, he turned the ignition key and edged back into traffic.

His words cut her in half as effectively as if he'd used a knife. Tears blurred her vision. She'd worked very hard to earn the money so that she could change her image. For the first time in her life, she had been enjoying herself and living life to the fullest. Just because he was a stick-in-the-mud, he expected her to follow his dull, dreary path. He wasn't being fair.

Unable to leave his last remark unchallenged, she asked, "What is that supposed to mean—that I looked a lot better to you when I was plain and poor?"

"If you don't know, there's no point discussing it. It's something you'll never understand." He pressed his lips together, and she knew she'd get nothing more from him.

How could she have let herself fall in love with a man who didn't understand her? Who made no effort to see her side of things or try to make her understand his. She sniffed and blinked.

As for their lovemaking, it had been a joyful experience that she'd cherish forever. No regrets. The memories would be stored in the mental album she'd started when she sold that first house, pressed between the same pages as the inflated palm tree and the calamine lotion. Then she'd flip to the next page. A sob lodged in her throat, but she choked it back. Turning that page would cut her as if the edges were razor sharp. But she would do it, because a lifetime in which to accumulate other memories loomed ahead of her.

Matt clutched the steering wheel and glanced at Tori. Her face was pinched and white. He felt bad, knowing he'd hurt her, but he couldn't do anything about it. She'd hurt him, too—and worse, disillusioned him. He'd continued to pursue her, believing she'd come to her senses once she became accustomed to her new wealth. He'd been sure her fascination with that shallow crowd was a temporary aberration.

How could she not realize that the people she thought of as revelers were really just a bunch of losers using her for their own gain? Becker was a total jerk, and he suspected that Clayborne was a crook. If she really expected to see any of her money again from that quarter, she was in for a big surprise.

Instead of getting angry, he should have let her float along in what she thought of as her bubble of happiness even though he knew it was going to burst. He didn't have to be the one to break it for her. She'd know the truth soon enough. But he was tired of waiting for her.

Then again, maybe he'd been wrong about her from the beginning. Maybe she really was just like her new friends. The ache in his heart made him catch his breath. Two days of lovemaking had merely whetted his appetite for more. Rationally, he knew it was time to let her go, but his heart and body already ached from losing her.

He regretted the silence that fell between them like the glass partition in the limousine, but he had nothing else to say to her. When he finally steered the car into the visitor's spot in front of her condo, he unloaded her things from the trunk and carried them to her front stoop. He waited to make sure she got inside safely, said a quiet "Good-bye," then got back into the car and drove away.

The moment Tori crossed her threshold, the

tears she'd been fighting began to fall. If only she'd followed her instincts about Matt, she wouldn't be hurting so badly now. She crossed her arms over her stomach. The pain was so intolerably bad.

If she'd stayed away from him, she reminded herself, she wouldn't have had those glorious two days to cherish for the rest of her life. If she'd known, would she have traded her present misery for those hours? No. She wouldn't have given them up for anything.

Her throat was so tight, she had trouble breathing. Yet she couldn't stop the tears. She simply couldn't understand why Matt was so angry. Why wouldn't he even talk to her? Explain? If he cared at all about their relationship, he would have discussed the problem. She sensed it went deeper than that stupid cruise, but he wouldn't tell her. She pulled a tissue out of a box, honked into it, then wiped her eyes with a dry corner.

What was she crying for? She had plenty of money and the potential to earn lots more. Her career was flourishing. So what if the man she had begun to think of as Mr. Right turned out not to be? Hadn't she been saying all along that she wasn't ready for him? Someday the right Mr. Right would come along.

She'd get over Matt. Someday. Maybe.

Until then, what was she going to do? She'd distract herself from her heartache with hard work. But, she realized, she didn't want anything more to do with Dain and his friends, not after Matt.

Not after finding out what getting the most out of life really meant. Not after finding and losing real, glorious love.

Chapter Fourteen

On Friday morning, Tori dragged herself into the office. Several appointments were scheduled for the weekend, and much as she would have preferred burying her head under her pillow for the rest of her life, Tori Gordon didn't do things like that. There were a lot of houses waiting to be bought and sold.

Irene started to greet her cheerfully, took one look at her face, then said a quiet "Good morning."

"Morning. Any messages?"

"Yeah." Irene handed her a stack of mail then leaned forward and whispered conspiratorially, "There was quite a hullabaloo yesterday. Brace yourself."

For a moment Tori wondered if somehow Irene and the others had heard what had happened between her and Matt. But, of course, only she, Tori, would have thought it was important.

Her interest was only slightly piqued. Shuffling

through the envelopes, she asked, "What happened?"

"Oh, I think I'll let Mr. Becker break it to you." Irene nodded at Dain who was just entering the office.

He brushed passed them. Even more than at his rude behavior, Tori was surprised at the way he looked. He wore a T-shirt rather than his usual crisp white shirt and tie. He was sitting at his desk now, his face buried in his hands. His shoulders were slumped in dejection.

"What's with him?"

"Go ask." The phone rang, and Irene swiveled back to her desk to answer it.

Tori went to Dain's desk and called his name. He looked up, groaned, and buried his head again. Hangover? she wondered.

"Too much partying?" she asked.

When he looked up again, she could see the pain in his green eyes, but they were clear, not bloodshot. He didn't seem to be hurting physically. This went much deeper.

Tori dropped into a chair. She had a sinking feeling that whatever was troubling him somehow affected her. "What is it?"

"The magazine."

"Something happen at the printers?" She held her breath.

"It never got to the printers."

"Why not?" she asked warily, knowing she really didn't want to hear the answer.

"Because that bastard Clayborne took off with

the money. There never was a magazine, Tori. He took my life savings, my dreams. My boat," Dain wailed. "Heaven knows where he is now."

"Oh, no! Have the police been called?"

"Sure. But by now he's probably having a grand old time spending my money on some remote island in the Bahamas, far from extradition. He'll be living high on the hog while I'll be chained to this damned desk for the rest of my life!" Dain slammed down his hand so hard that the telephone jingled and the plastic stationery tray rattled.

Tori felt little sympathy for him. After all, he was the one who had introduced her to Ellis Clayborne in the first place. It was on his recommendation that she'd invested her money.

Matt would have a field day with this. "Don't tell Matt."

"Tell Matt!" Is that all you care about? I'm ruined and all you can think about is your precious boyfriend. Go away." He waved his hand. "Leave me alone."

As she hurried away, she saw with dismay that Wendy was already waiting for her, sitting by her desk. Tori was sorely tempted to turn the other way and stroll right out the door. Instead, she squared her shoulders and walked straight ahead.

"Hi," she said with false cheerfulness.

"Good morning, Tori. I see Dain's been telling you about Ellis Clayborne's disappearing act. I hope you didn't give him too much money."

"Did you?" Tori hedged. She knew the other

woman's claws were already unsheathed, ready to pounce.

"Not a dime. Matt advised against it. And since I placed my trust in him as my financial advisor, I had no choice but to listen to him. You should have, too."

Holier-than-thou hypocrite, Tori thought. Wendy just wanted to rub her nose in her mistake. Yet the woman's words hit her like a one-two punch, knocking understanding into her. Not following Matt's advice implied that she didn't trust him—professionally or personally. No wonder he took it so hard.

A smug smile marred Wendy's beautiful face. Why did Wendy dislike her so much? For a little while, when Wendy had sold the Boca Raton house, Tori thought her attitude might be changing.

"What's with you?" Tori demanded. "What have I ever done to you?"

Wendy jerked back and widened her eyes. "Nothing."

"Then why are you always so nasty and sarcastic to me?"

"I . . . I," Wendy stammered. "I didn't realize . . ."

"Of course you realized." All the anger and hurt she'd experienced from Wendy's acid tongue, coupled with her pain at her breakup with Matt, and her embarrassment at the foolishness of her investment, came pouring out. "Every word you uttered was calculated to hurt me."

Wendy started to get up. "I don't have to take this."

"Yes, you do. Just like I had to put up with all your garbage."

Marginally aware that everyone in the office was gaping at them, Tori grasped Wendy's arm. Although Wendy resisted and sputtered all the way, Tori steered her into the coffe-break room, slammed the door, and turned the lock. With her back against the door, she faced Wendy, ready for the coming battle.

"Move over." Wendy lunged and tried to push her aside. "I'm getting out of here."

Tori held her ground. "Not till I'm through talking to you."

Wide-eyed, her mouth open, Wendy backed off and stared at her, for once at a loss for words.

Tori said, "That day, after I sold the Palmworth mansion, you knew I was in the rest room. You knew exactly what you were doing when you called me a frumpy, drab little mouse. You were cruel. Deliberately cruel!" She felt the hurt as keenly as she had that day. Tears stung her eyes as she relived the memory. She blinked them away, letting anger carry her.

"I didn't know you were there," Wendy wailed.

At Tori's skeptical look, Wendy added meekly, "Not for sure."

"I had the most wonderful revenge, though," Tori said, her voice now dripping with saccharine. "Thanks to what I overheard you say, I decided to change my image."

270

"What I said?"

"Yeah. Thanks to you I realized I had fallen into a rut, and the time to climb out of it was long overdue." She had the satisfaction of seeing Wendy wince.

When she didn't speak, Tori continued, "I could never figure out why you wanted to hurt me. I never did anything to you. So why did you treat me that way?"

Wendy studied her for a moment, then replied, "I knew Matt Claussen was attracted to you. I wanted him for myself and—"

"Attracted to me?" That's what Matt had said. "To frumpy, mousy me? Come on, Wendy, you can do better than that."

"I was jealous and hurt that he wouldn't give me a tumble. I wanted to get back at you. Didn't you see the way he looked at you?"

"After I made all that money and dyed my hair and bought beautiful clothes, he suddenly took an interest in me, yeah. But you were picking on me even before that."

Wendy shook her head. "I never thought you were stupid, but I've changed my mind. The man had the hots for you since he first laid eyes on you, but you just kept giving him the cold shoulder. I couldn't stand it. Here was this gorgeous hunk, practically drooling over you, and you wouldn't give him the time of day. I would have sold my soul for a night with him."

Tori turned away. Matt had insisted that he'd asked her out many times, yet she still found it hard to believe. "You're crazy. No one looked at me until I changed by image. Even Dain—"

Wendy was laughing now. "Dain wouldn't have cared if you wore a burlap sack and had a face uglier than a Halloween witch's. He was after your money." The words were spoken honestly without a hint of malice.

Tori knew, had always known, the truth of those words. She moved away from the door and dropped into a chair. All the fight had left her. Although her pride was stung, Dain's duplicity couldn't hurt her because she didn't care about Dain and never had.

With a sigh, she looked up at Wendy and saw her through different eyes. She no longer seemed malicious. She was just a woman whose jealousy had gotten the better of her.

Tori shrugged. "I guess in a way Dain and I were using each other."

Wendy filled two mugs with coffee, put one on the table in front of Tori, and took the chair across from her. "Are you finished with him?"

Sipping her coffee, Tori lifted one shoulder. "Since there really wasn't anything to begin with, there's nothing to be finished with."

"What about Matt?" Wendy's eyes gleamed and seemed to bore into her.

Trying to keep her gaze level and open, Tori asked, "What about him?"

"Are you two an item?"

Tori thought for a minute. What should her answer be? They certainly weren't an item—not any longer. Yet she didn't want to give Wendy her blessing to make another play for Matt.

"It's hard to say" was the reply she finally made.

Obviously dissatisfied with that answer, Wendy turned up a corner of her mouth in an expression that looked more like a grimace than a grin. When she spoke, it was a complete change of subject that once again threw Tori off balance.

"So how much money did you lose in Becker and Clayborne's scheme?"

"Moneywise, not much. But—" She broke off before she let slip that she'd lost Matt.

"But enough?" Wendy finished for her. "I suppose that cruise is off."

For a moment, the pleasures of sailing through the open sea with Matt flashed through Tori's mind. But he didn't want to go on her cruise, so what was the point of chartering the yacht? Without Matt, it wouldn't be any fun at all.

"Yeah, it's off," she said.

"I don't blame you. I'd do it myself, but I don't have your kind of money—not yet, anyway. Look. I'm glad we talked this out. How about a truce?" Wendy suggested. "I'm sorry I hurt you."

Tori took the hand she offered. "Sure. It'll be a lot more pleasant working here if I know I don't have to watch my back."

Wendy smiled. "I was that bad, huh?"

"You know you were."

Someone knocked on the door. "Are you two okay in there?" It was Irene's voice.

Tori got up to turn the lock. Immediately, Irene

poked her head into the room. "Are you both alive?"

"Yes."

"And we've made up," Wendy said, coming to join them. "I've promised to be a good girl from now on. You know, Tori, we should consider forming a partnership. Together, we'd be quite a force in this business."

Tori hedged. Despite the conciliatory words, it would be a long time, if ever, before she would trust Wendy. "I'm not ready to work with anyone yet. Maybe. . . ." She allowed the suggestion to drift off.

Ignoring the curious stares of their colleagues, Tori returned to her desk. If Wendy wanted to gossip about what had passed between them, it was her business. Some day she might tell Irene herself, but right now she had a stack of messages to sort through.

During what was left of the morning she made appointments, arranged for ads she had thought she wouldn't need since she was planning to advertise in Ellis's publication, and generally tried to clear her desk of some of the work that had piled up while she was with Matt in the Keys. Every time she heard the switchboard ring, her heart jumped and she looked up, hoping Irene would signal that Matt was calling. But he didn't, just as she'd expected.

It was really over between them. That had been clear yesterday. Why would she think anything had changed overnight? But he was still her financial

274

advisor. She brightened a bit. He couldn't ignore her completely.

One of his responsibilities was to report the status of her investments. He'd have to call her to discuss business. Maybe she'd drop into his office now and then to subtly remind him of what they'd shared and what he was missing. Given time, she'd win him back. Her optimism kept her buoyed just enough to maintain a normal facade.

After lunch at her desk, a carton of yogurt and an orange which she barely touched, Irene brought over a fax and handed it to her. Tori scanned it. From Matt. Her spirits, already hovering just above floor level, sunk.

She'd forgotten they could conduct their business without actually talking to each other. There would be no phone calls or face-to-face business meetings in his office.

The last trace of optimism fled her heart. A dreary, dark cloud circled her head like a flock of vultures.

The wound in her soul, barely closed, far from healed, burst apart, leaving an open, bleeding gash. She passed her hand over her face, and her hot tears scalded her cold palms. Now she knew with certainty she had lost Matt forever.

Tori knew curious eyes were watching her. She didn't care. Yet she needed to be alone and sought the relative privacy of the rest room. She flung herself onto the vinyl couch set into a small recess and leaned back against the tile wall. Struggling for breath, she pressed her hand to her face and fought the tears that tumbled over her fingers.

After several minutes, when she could inhale without her throat tightening painfully, she felt she had gained some control over her emotions. That was when she realized Matt's fax was still clutched in her fist. Earlier, giving it a cursory glance, she'd noticed something about a stock. Curious now, she smoothed the wrinkled page on her knee and began to read.

The message explained that one of the stocks he had bought for her was plummeting in value. Did she want to sell it before it dropped even lower or hold on to it because most likely it would rebound? If she would sign the attached memo and fax it back, he would sell. Otherwise he'd hold on to it.

Anger clutched her like the tentacles of an octopus and squeezed out the last of her tears. She balled the note and tossed it in the trash can. So Mr. Perfect fouled up!

He was Mr. Perfect, she conceded. Faults and all he was her Mr. Perfect. And she wanted him back.

She walked over to the sink and shuddered when she saw her red, swollen eyes in the mirror. She splashed cold water on her face, did a quick patch up job to her makeup, then put on her dark, concealing sunglasses.

Ignoring the stares from her colleagues, she raised her chin and went back to her desk. She grabbed the phone and punched in Matt's number. When he came on the line, she said without preamble, "I thought everything you recommended was foolproof! You said I had to invest my money so that I'd get a good income. I didn't need your advice in order to lose money. I did that all by myself." She bit her tongue. He'd find out about Ellis soon enough.

"I heard Clayborne took a powder. I'm sorry."

"That doesn't defend what you did. You were supposed to make me money, not lose it." Her anger masked her pain. She'd wanted to hear his voice, but not this impersonal, businesslike tone.

"Any investment is speculation. You know that, Tori. But some things are more sure than others."

"Like the stock market?" she chided.

"Like knowing what you're doing, and who you're doing it with."

He certainly wasn't talking about stocks and bonds.

"And I suppose you know what you're doing all the time? You're always right?" She had to prod and poke him to make him bleed as much as she was.

"Not always. Sometimes I'm so wrong that I begin to doubt my own intelligence. I'm sorry about the stock, Tori. What do you want to do? I think it'll go up again once the panic stops." He sounded so lethargic — as if he didn't care. "It's a good solid stock and has paid a regular dividend for the past ten years. But I did feel you had the right to make the decision."

"Sell it!" she exclaimed and slammed down the phone.

She couldn't stay in the office another minute. She had to get away. Had to think. Had to figure out a way to make him see that what they'd shared was special and shouldn't be thrown away. She had to show him how much she loved him.

When the phone crashed in Matt's ear, he saw red. He'd done his best for her, then, when he made one little miscalculation, she was angry. And he deserved it, he conceded, feeling the anger seep out of him. He'd been cocky and self-assured. He wasn't as perfect as he wanted to believe. The money she'd lost following his advice wasn't that much less than the amount she wanted to spend on the cruise.

But it had been wonderful hearing her voice. For the first time in twenty-four hours, he smiled, remembering her whispered words and exciting moans during their lovemaking. Leaning back in his chair, he propped his feet on an open desk drawer.

He'd sent the fax instead of phoning her because he didn't want to hear her anger. When she spoke, he wanted to hear the sweetness in her voice that made him think of arias and nightingales—and wedding bells.

And suddenly he realized that in his mind she was Tori, that he'd actually called her by her preferred nickname. To him, her transformation was complete. She'd become the woman she wanted to be.

He'd told her the truth when he said he liked the old Victoria. She was there somewhere, mingling with the new Tori—the woman he loved. He was sure of it.

He had to find a way to bring her back. If he gave up on her, it was like giving up on himself. He wanted to spend the rest of his life with her—with the real sweet and passionate woman. He wanted to be able to call her Victoria again.

He must do something before she got away from him. Putting his hands behind his head, he closed his eyes, the position in which he did his best thinking. He discarded one idea after another. At last, he opened his eyes and dropped his feet to the floor with a thud. He had come up with a great plan.

He pulled back his leg and flipped onto his back. "You're no Victoria Nightingale, that's for sure.

Chapter Fifteen

He'd called her Tori!

The realization hit her with the force of a tidal wave. It rolled over her. Swamped her. Made her feel as if she were drowning. Ever since she'd changed her image, she'd been trying to get Matt to call her by her nickname. It represented all she wished she could be.

His use of Tori proved that she'd gotten her wish.

It was a hollow victory. Without him, her life was washing away with the receding tide. That wish should never have come true.

Matt preferred the woman she used to be, that was why he always called her Victoria. Now, when she'd lost him, Tori realized that more than the money she thought would bring joy to her fun-starved heart, more than anything in the whole world, she loved Matt Claussen.

And she knew just what she needed to do to make everything right again. No more wishes. Just action.

After one quick stop at the supermarket, she drove straight home and headed for the shower. Later, after styling her hair, she rummaged through her closet until, way in the back, she found the dress she was looking for and slipped it on. The phone rang just as she was stepping into the matching low-heeled pumps. One shoe on, one off, she went to pick up the receiver.

When she heard Matt's voice, her heart began thudding as if it were trying to beat its way out of her chest.

"Will you meet me at the marina on the Lake Trail?" he asked.

That was where they'd strolled after she'd paid off her bet and bought him dinner—where the love between them had blossomed. In her mind, the Lake Trail was magical, the only place in the world where they might be able to work out their differences. Did he feel that way too?

"Why?" she asked.

"Because I want to see you. Because we need to talk. Because, well, because I have a plan."

Tori felt her lips curve up in a grin. From happy experience, she knew what tended to happen when Matt had a plan. This particular plan seemed to be falling in well with her own schemes. If he'd called five minutes later, she'd have been in her car, heading for his office.

"When do you want to meet?"

"Can you leave now?"

For a split second she considered putting him off for a bit. But what was the point of being coy or playing hard to get? "As soon as I put on my other shoe, I'll be out the door."

"I'll be waiting," he replied before hanging up.

She drove fast, yet seemed to catch every red light. Road construction slowed the already inching rush hour traffic, making her want to scream with frustration. At last the bridge to Palm Beach was straight ahead. Her stomach clenched from a mixture of anticipation and anxiety. Her meeting with Matt was so near now. When the drawbridge started to rise in front of her, she jammed on her brakes and pounded on the steering wheel. Was the whole of Florida conspiring to keep her from Matt?

When she finally crossed into Palm Beach, a vacant parking space near the Lake Trail beckoned to her. Taking the convenient spot as a good omen, she got out. So intent on finding Matt, she was barely aware of the thick, muggy late afternoon heat. She crossed the grassy area near the parking lot and walked onto the blacktopped trail.

Her steps were slow. After rushing in slow motion, fighting obstacles to her progress, she couldn't make herself hurry. What if Matt wanted to end their relationship once and for all? Even turn her business over to someone else? Impossible. If that was the case, he would have communicated his intent by sending another one of those blasted faxes. No. He really wanted what she wanted—to make things right between them.

Then she saw him, and her steps faltered.

Matt couldn't believe his eyes. The woman coming toward him looked like Tori, yet she didn't. His heart lurched and thudded against his ribs. The wind had caught her brown hair and was pulling tendrils from the tight chignon. What had she done to herself?

And she was having a helluva time trying to keep the full skirt of her blue dress from blowing immodestly high. He remembered when, in the Keys, she'd struggled against the wind to keep her skirt down and her hair away from her face. The magic of that evening came back to him with a wave of longing and regret. If only he could have that vacation to do over. He'd make sure it ended very differently.

He waved and hurried toward her. As the distance between them narrowed, he recognized the dress she was wearing as the first one she'd bought after she'd sold the big house. He remembered that she'd worn it on their lunch date at the Pink Shrimp. At the time, he'd regretted its unfashionable length because it hid too much of her leg. Yet the silky fabric had highlighted her curves in a most provocative manner.

"What have you done?" he asked, touching her dark bun.

"You wanted Victoria . . ."

He kissed the top of her head. "You liked your hair blond and your pretty clothes." One at a time, he pulled out the pins that anchored her sleek hairstyle. With the help of the wind, her waves were soon whipping across her shoulders. A

283

hand on either side of her face, he pushed the curls back and kept them out of her eyes. "I liked them, too. You shouldn't give them up to please me." Their gazes locked, and Tori felt their souls unite.

"I will if you want me to," she said breathlessly.

"I want whatever will make you happy," he said. "Rather than considering your needs, I expected you to change. I wanted you to give up your new lifestyle. I'm sorry. That was unfair of me."

"But you were right."

Matt grimaced and released her. "No I wasn't."

Since he'd dropped her off last night, he'd done a lot of soul-searching. He'd realized there were a lot of things about Tori he preferred to the old Victoria. He loved her laugh, and her optimistic nature. She made him relax and have fun. Without the need to prove that he was as fun-loving as Becker, he'd never have improvised that indoor beach party. He wouldn't have taken her down to the Keys and learned what making love really meant.

She'd made him see there was a lot he'd been missing since he'd moved to Florida and glued his nose to the grindstone. He hadn't even made the time to go surfing. He couldn't wait to teach her.

"You were right about me," Tori protested. "I was shallow and stupid." She wished she could probe his mind and know if she was truly reaching him. "I wasn't thinking straight."

He shook his head. "I was pompous and bossy." She felt his finger tremble against her cheek.

284

She grimaced in self-disgust. "I was such a fool, chasing rainbows that didn't exist, willing to throw away the possibility of a future with—" She broke off. Matt had never spoken about a future together, never spoken of love. But it had been there in his eyes, in every gesture. In his touch. One of them had to be the first to say it.

"—with the man I love."

He touched her lip. "Am I that man?"

"Yes, oh yes." Longing to be in his arms, she swayed toward him and waited for him to hold her.

Instead, he took her hand and started leading her to the marina. "Come on. I want to show you something."

This "something" was part of his plan, she knew. Excited to find out what he was up to, she let him pull her along.

Ahead of them, several vessels—yachts, ketches, cabin cruisers—were bobbing in their slips. Had he rented a yacht? Was that his plan?

Matt pointed and she noticed a sleek sailboat, its sails furled on tall masts. How wonderful, she thought. They were going sailing.

"What do you think of her?" he asked.

"She's beautiful. Looks like the one we saw behind your house the other night."

He squinted into the lowering suns. "So it does." He was still holding her hand, so all he had to do was give it a little tug to urge her onto the dock where the boat was moored.

As they drew closer, she saw the name painted

285

in deep blue against the sparkling white of the hull.

Victoria G.

"Matt," she exclaimed. "You didn't."

"Of course I did. Aren't you worth it?"

"Now where have I heard that before?" she asked, then nodded. *"We're* worth it." *We,* she mused. It had a nice solid ring to it.

"That's not all."

"Oh?"

"Let's go on our boat, and I'll show you."

What could possibly top his buying that sailboat and naming it for her? she thought as she clambered onto the wooden deck of the *Victoria G.* Although he still hadn't said the words, his gift proved that he loved her. She was filled with joy. She wanted to lurch into his arms, but he was fumbling for something in his back pocket.

Finally, Matt handed her a jeweler's box, like the one that had held her palm tree pin. Now that she knew he could be totally unpredictable, she had no idea what to expect. A sailboat pin would be almost too trite.

"Aren't you going to open it?"

She was enjoying the anticipation too much to end it so quickly. She toyed with the lid. "I don't have anything for you this time."

"You don't? What about the brown hair and the blue dress? They're wonderful gifts that tell me how much I mean to you." He kissed her gently on the lips. "I love you. I should have told you sooner."

Her heart took wing, soaring high above her elusive rainbow. She bounced the box in her hand.

"Open it," he ordered.

She flipped back the top. A diamond trapped the sun and refracted little rainbows against the blue velvet of the box. Tori's breath caught. An engagement ring. If it had been a paper cigar band, it wouldn't have meant any less to her. She loved the ring because Matt had given it to her.

His eyes glittering like the jewel, Matt took out the ring. "Will you wear it? Will you marry me?"

In response, she gave him her left hand. He had to hold it tight to keep it from trembling as he slipped the ring on her third finger.

"Yes, Matt. I'll marry you." Now she had riches beyond any she'd wished for or dreamed about. She loved Matt, and he loved her. What more could any woman want?

"As soon as we're married, we'll change the name of the boat to the *Victoria C.* All I'll have to do is paint out the crossline in the G."

"I love you, Matt," she whispered.

"I love you, too. Because we love each other, our rainbow does exist. We've found the pot of gold, Victoria. As long as we're together." At last, he took her in his arms.

Victoria! She returned his ardent kisses.

He had called her Victoria.